I0624975

Panic in Year 2020: A Zombie Novel

Ro Van Saint

Z2R Media

www.zerotorockstar.com

© 2013, Ro Van Saint
Cover Art: Ro Van Saint
September 2013

This is a work of fiction. Similarities to persons, living or dead, events, or locales, is purely coincidental.

All rights reserved. No part of this book may be reproduced, in any form, or by any means, without the permission of the author.

Other Titles

Bad Juju: Volume 1
Bad Juju: Volume 2
Primer: A Zombie Short Story
Degeneration: A Post-Apocalyptic Novella
A Strange Occurrence on Keystone Drive
Sid Valentine
Ghost Town

Prologue: Space is the Place

Captain's Journal 7/17/2021:

We are approaching Earth finally. I'm a little afraid what we'll find when we land. Haven't heard from anyone in months. Not from Mission Control. Not from family. No transmission from any of the stations that we've tried tapping into. We'd get the usual static but no more. The crew's morale - well, it's as expected. They all have people they've left behind back home. The stress of not knowing why we can't get a hold of anyone has gotten to even the toughest of the crew. I've tried my best to show a strong front but they know me better than that. Being in close quarters with a small group of people, working and living side by side for ten years, they become your world. We are expecting to touch down in approximately 24 hours. We've ran through multiple simulations of scenarios and drills to prepare for the post landing contact. We'll reassess the situation then as needed.

Captain Toller Lee and his crew have been on this mission since 2010. Normally a day like this is a day for celebration but the uncertainty of what awaited them was unnerving. Sleep amongst the crew had been scarce in the months that followed the last live feed they received. Most got by with less than three hours of sleep per day. A crew of seven moody and half-awake space officers trying to operate a sophisticated ship was a very scary thought. Toller had finally stepped in and enforced a daily mandatory rest period, the adult version of the mid-afternoon nap time that kindergarten kids would take. The announcement wasn't received well but the intention was understood.

They all gathered in the mess hall, the smell of freshly brewed coffee permeated everything. Ketan Murphy - the chief science officer, shuffled a deck of cards and started setting up for a quick game of solitaire. Eugene "Mech" Adams, the engineer slash mechanic slash ultimate gearhead was busy constructing a multi-layered sandwich made of tomatoes, alfalfa sprouts, and cucumbers grown on the ship. Out of one of the latched drawers he pulled out what looked to be, at first glance, a tube of unmarked toothpaste, space mayonnaise or something that resembled it. He flipped the cap open and squeezed the contents on top of his sandwich before slapping down flat bread on top of it. Mech took a giant bite out of his towering creation.

"Seriously, first thing I'm gonna do is to eat some real food," Mech muttered in between chews as he sat down on the bench next to Ketan. "Well, maybe not the first thing." He smirked and nudged Ketan who looked mildly annoyed.

"A decade of eating rations disguised as food and getting pussy from the same women is causing irreparable damage to my well-being. I'm gonna need therapy after this and some serious pampering." He took another bite and wiped the imitation mayo off the corners of his mouth with his sleeve.

Ingrid Laszcek walked by and overheard the crude comment by Mech.

"Hey, asshole, it's not like you're my first choice either. But beggars can't be choosers.

Besides, I've had better." She sat directly across Ketan with a cup of coffee in her hand.

"It sure sounded like you enjoyed yourself the other night though. Can't fake that kinda shit up ya know." He winked at her.

"I can't believe you're up here, acting and talking the way you do," Ketan said without looking up. He'd won another round of solitaire and was now gathering the playing cards into a stack.

"Acting like what?"

"Like a knucklehead, is what."

"You know what your problem is? You take everything so damn seriously. And you think you're better than everyone. Lighten the fuck up will ya? Don't be bitter because I get more tail than you do." He took another bite of the sandwich.

Ketan shook his head as he shuffled the playing cards. He played it cool, not showing any type of frustration when truthfully all he wanted to do was bash Mech's face in, sandwich and all. He set up another round of solitaire as he glanced up to look at Ingrid who was reading from her MV (media viewer).

He and Ingrid had a thing during the early days of this voyage. Not just a sex-thing but a little more serious than that. With all the work this job entailed it just never fully developed somehow. It wasn't exactly the main priority here. As time went on, everyone in this ship pretty much has had some type of intimate relationship with each other. It was just the nature of the job. It got awfully lonely up here. Ketan was bitter and angry that he never told her that he didn't want her sleeping with Mech or anyone else for that matter. He wanted her all to himself but he didn't have the nerve to tell her that. And besides, what if he did tell her and she went ahead and disregarded it and slept around anyway? It was just more humiliating that way.

They'll be home soon and he'll have the opportunity to pursue this the way he should have done so in the beginning. Just him and Ingrid. That's what he kept telling himself.

Capt. Lee entered the mess hall with First Officer Natalie Jones, lead pilot, the captain's wingman.

Trailing them were Dr. Joyce Glenn and his wife Dr. Karen Sol, the real brains of the crew. They had a combined total of five doctorates between the two of them. Certified geniuses and swingers to boot. Just ask Mech. Toller had a very serious official look on his face as usual. He never broke character. He was the captain and he needed to project the image of a fearless leader. Everyone at the table started to stand up.

"At ease, go about your business, I'm just here for coffee and a quick chat," Toller poured coffee into two large cups, one for himself, the other for his wingman. The evil genius couple already had a couple of small cartons of milk and sat down next to Ingrid.

The captain positioned himself at the head of the table, took a big gulp out of his drink, and tapped his left hand fingers repeatedly on the surface of the table, one by one from pinky to thumb, a nervous habit he's had since grade school. Everyone remained quiet waiting in anticipation for him to say something. The awkward silence built the tension up to an uncomfortable level.

"I'd really love to have a cigarette," Toller casually said, putting forth his best effort to creating small talk. It was obvious how stressed he was. He's aged quite a bit since the beginning of this trip. A lot more grays peppered his short dark hair. Even his light scruffy beard had traces of it. The dark circles under his eyes made him appear to be older than he was, the weight loss gave his face a gaunt, sickly appearance and now his clothing looked one size larger which made him look even thinner.

"A cigarette, a large order of Lo Mein from Chen Garden's take out from my neighborhood and a large cup of soda halfway filled with ice."

"Damn, that sounds real good Cap," Mech said before he chugged down a mouthful of bottled water.

"So, what's everybody's plans when we get home?" Toller asked the crew. He tried to steer clear from talking about what they could be coming home to. Something's not right, and he knew it. They all knew it.

"Oh, not much really, just wanna get some rest and do normal civilian things, you know." Ketan shuffled the pack of cards one last time and placed it in a pile, lining up all the edges as he did so.

Natalie, now sitting next to Mech, responded to Toller's prompt.

"I'm gonna take a nice long bath, put on some comfy pajamas and sleep for days."

"I'll have to ditto that one, only in my version I'll be eating Rocky Road ice cream in bed and watching old reruns of Alfred Hitchcock Presents," Ingrid finally chimed in.

Capt. Lee looked as if he was starting to relax a bit as he listened in. Glenn and Sol acted as stuffy as ever, displaying a textbook definition of prim and proper. The captain turned his attention to them and tried to include them in the conversation.

"How about you guys, any special plans when we get home?"

Dr. Glenn was first to answer.

"That all depends on what we find when we get home, doesn't it?"

Ketan and Mech glared at him with fiery eyes. How dare he bring this moment down? Everyone knew that Capt. Lee was just trying to help everyone cope. Lighten the mood some before having to deal with reality.

"The fact is we have had no contact with Mission Control or anyone down below in the last nine months. The intranet site that was meant to keep us updated with news and events had not been updated. The private com-line that we used to talk with friends and family had been transmitting nothing but static signals. Any other attempts to hack into other possible lines of communication have failed. This all happened right after that storm. Deny it all you want, refuse to acknowledge it if you wish, but you remember what Carl had told us a week prior to the storm's arrival. He said that they were preparing for an upcoming storm and it looked pretty severe from the satellite images. You've seen it yourselves. The size of it was slightly larger than the North American continent. And when it finally hit, it kept coming and lasted for a week. Shortly after that was when all the lines were severed. Who knows what we'll be coming home to?"

"I'd have to agree with him. I think it's best to expect the worse and go from there," Sol said, standing by her man.

Toller gave Mech, Ingrid, Ketan, and Natalie a stern look as if to say I've got this handled, bite your tongue.

"We've already gone over the landing procedures numerous times, we're as prepared as we're ever going to get. There's no definite way of preparing for the unknown. We are all trained professionals with backgrounds and expertise in various areas and if we all keep our heads together, keep our cool, communicate effectively, that's as best as it's going to get. I am confident with everyone's skills and capabilities, and I'm just looking forward to being home again."

Toller had his doubts about his mini-speech. He partly agreed with Glenn and Sol but refused to openly say so. The rest of his crew needed him on their side. But truth be told, Toller had a bad feeling about the whole thing.

**

The Homecoming

Captain's Journal 7/18/2021:

We are currently orbiting Earth in preparation for the reentry. I don't foresee any difficulties with the entry and the actual landing. The satellite imagery is non-functional but we can visibly see that there doesn't seem to be any type of storm clouds hovering around where we need to be. The initial plan of action is to attempt to make contact as soon as we touch down. Surely we'll be able to scan multiple frequencies and reach someone. Officers Murphy, Laszcek and I will then make the trek back to the main building to check out the premises. The rest will remain on the ship until further notice from us. Their main focus is to establish communication with anyone they can reach and to keep a close eye on what we're doing. Pending clearance from me, Mech and Natalie will proceed to secure a vehicle and explore the secondary buildings surrounding the perimeter. Dr. Glenn and Sol will resume com-line duties and await further instructions. If anything should happen to me, First Officer Jones will take over as Captain; the crew is expected to follow her orders.

The main compartment was busy with activity as the crew of Atlas II prepared for landing. Glenn and Sol were already strapped into their seats and analyzing data on their MV. Mech double checked the settings on the panel in front of him before locking in the harness into his seat. Ingrid was across from him, also monitoring the figures flashing on the screen in front of her. Ketan is situated to Ingrid's immediate right, looking very intense as he tweaked the controls on his designated dashboard. Natalie was already at the helm, cool and collected as ever with that determined look on her face that everyone relied upon in times of crisis (and Lord knows they've had plenty of those in the decade they've all been together). The captain may have been their appointed leader but Natalie was their rock. She was the unshakeable force that barely said anything but when she did open her mouth to address the group, everyone listened and was instantly moved to do better.

Toller made his way towards the front, patting everyone on the shoulders as he passed by, a ritual he's kept since the early days of training. He wasn't big on speeches, thought it was pointless to punctuate an event with words. He thought that the event itself should be enough. So in typical Toller fashion he said nothing. Natalie looked over wishing he HAD said something, anything. This strong and silent leader bit wasn't what the crew needed right now. She hated that she was always the one that had to say the right things, always had to lift them up and push them forward. What about her? Who was there to lift her up as she sat scared shitless and a messed up bundle of nerves? Yet she had to string the right words together and be strong because they needed her to be strong. She knew how everyone looked up to her and relied on her unwavering will. They told her all the time. Not in so many words but they did tell her. Natalie closed her eyes momentarily, took a deep breath and swiveled her chair around to face the crew.

"Alright, listen up...for ten years we have worked and lived side by side, this ship had been our home and this voyage our life. It hasn't always been easy but we made it work. Nine months ago we've lost contact with not only Mission Control but with everyone and everything else down there. So once again we find ourselves treading unknown territory. There's no telling what awaits us when we touch down. But as always we will endure. Let's go home, shall we?"

"Fuck, yeah! Let's do this!" Mech said, his hands displayed the universal sign for devil horns rock and roll style.

They sat back and braced themselves for reentry.

**

Landing strip, CTX Space Center

It was a rough and bumpy descent but they made it. The ship rattled and shook the whole way down like a tin can full of marbles. The crew of Atlas II lucked out yet again. All corresponding body parts still attached to its appropriate owner. In this field, most would say that's a good day. Silence in the cabin as everyone realized they just dodged yet another bullet. Surely their luck was bound to run out soon. But for now, they reveled in the accomplishment.

"Shit yeah, baby! Nothing turns me on more than a smooth entry," Mech boasted as he unclicked his belt.

"Fuckin'-eh, just once I wish you'd shut your mouth and act right." Ketan shook his head.

"Man, we just came home from a long-ass excursion, we survived that nearly impossible reentry and all you can do is bitch me out. Well, you know what? You can just fuck off!" Mech stepped up to Ketan, their faces about an inch apart from each other.

"Boy, you need to back off or I will hurt you," Ketan said as he stared right back at Mech with unblinking furious eyes.

"That is it! Enough! I ain't your momma so I'm not gonna say it again. Stand back or I will sort both of you out, do you fucking understand?" Captain Toller Lee addressed the two men with a loud booming voice that none of the crew had ever heard. The Captain meant it, you could just see in the way he stood and looked at them. Ketan and Mech eased on up from each other's personal space.

"Everyone knows what they need to do right now so let's proceed. Let's stick to the plan and find out what we've been missing. Ketan and Ingrid, get your gear together and let's head out, and the rest of you keep in touch. Will I have to find a babysitter for you Mech?" Toller was already on his way out.

"No Cap. Glenn and Sol will do," Mech answered back with a wink.

Toller made his way down the short corridor that led to the exterior chamber flanked by Ingrid and Ketan, the hatch already open and the ramp down. Their com-line was open to all available frequencies, and each carried a light backpack with a survival and emergency kit.

"Welcome home, crew."

And with that, Toller set his first steps on Earth for the first time in ten years.

**

The first thing they noticed was the smell. It was like when you travelled from one country to another, there was a distinct scent to each place. A smell that couldn't be categorized in the good or bad department, it was just different.

But this odor, it was subtle and had a foulness to it. Like something rotten baking out in the heat of the sun for days.

The sun beamed and lit everything within its reach in a bright washed out yellow. The heat felt intensely warm on their skin, a sensation they haven't experienced in a decade.

Then there was the stillness of it all. So far they saw no movement from anywhere. No breeze. No employees driving around in between buildings in golf carts. No sounds of traffic here or above.

Captain Toller Lee had only started to be concerned a few minutes ago when they received no signals even with the ship at a complete stop. All they were able to pick up was static. He felt his gut turn just a little then. Something was seriously wrong here but he didn't want to alarm the crew. In the few minutes they've been out walking towards the main building, the concern turned into a nervous anxiety that he couldn't shake off.

"We are now entering the Southwest wing of the main building, give me a status report Atlas." Toller paused just outside the tinted glass door as he waited for a response from Atlas II.

"Com-line is actively scanning all available frequencies sir, with no luck so far. Want us to head off to the support buildings, cap?" Mech answered back, eagerly wanting to explore with the cool kids.

"Negative on that for the meantime. We're headed inside right now. Someone's bound to be here and when we find that someone we'll get some answers. In the meantime hold your post and keep trying with the com-line. You guys good otherwise?" Toller was already in the building, Ketan and Ingrid right behind him.

"Yes, we're good, keep us updated." Mech sounded like a kid that was just told by a parent that he wasn't allowed to play outside with his friends.

**

Ingrid approached a desk and picked up the phone. She first dialed the number to her parents' house. No answer. She tried her sister's cell and work number. No answer there either. She looked back to the guys and shook her head. Ketan grabbed the phone from her and tried some of his contacts which resulted in the same outcome.

"You wanna try Cap?" Ketan offered the phone to Toller.

"No, we need to keep moving." Toller didn't have anyone to call that would want to hear from him. His ex-wife divorced him eight years ago. He received an e-mail about it in space. They didn't have any children together. He had not been in contact with any family member in years except for his brother, Cormac. Even that was infrequent. His work was his life.

The large digital clock on the wall indicated that it was 3:15pm CST, Wednesday. Midafternoon right smack in the middle of the week and no one was here to work. Most of the work areas looked orderly, no signs of struggle. The scent was stronger in here. They went down the hallway and checked each room they passed. Toller veered to the left and punched in the access code. He was headed towards the chief of staff's office. If anyone should be here, it would be Carl, another guy married to his work. Carl's office was vacant, his desk looked slightly disheveled with some papers scattered on the floor. Toller did a quick walk-through of the office then picked up the phone. He dialed Carl's cell number, the one for emergency calls. The man owned two mobile phones. One for personal and work. The other for very urgent calls such as highly classified related cases and calls from one of his mistresses. After several rings he expected the voicemail to pick up but instead someone at the other end clicked over.

"Hello? Hello? Hey, Carl! It's me, Toller, I'm in your office, Atlas II is home, we're all here, what the hell is going on? Everyone's just disap---"

A groan. Whoever picked up the line uttered a low groan. Then another one.

"Hello? Who is this? Listen, I need to speak to Carl Mendelson. Put him on the line."

"Uurg, ech, ech, errr, rrrwarr..."

The groan had turned into some sort of a growl. Even Ingrid and Ketan heard it now.

"Holy shit." Toller looked at the receiver in disbelief and threw it on the desk.

"What the hell was that?" Ketan stumbled back and nearly tripped on Ingrid.

"I don't know. I don't think we should be here right now." Toller stormed out of the room in a hurried rush.

Mech's voice broke through the ear buds they all wore.

"Hey guys, we picked something up from the com-line. We couldn't figure out who it was. Sounded like a person's voice but..." Mech trailed off and let the words just hang there.

"But what Mech?" Ketan asked, his breath short and jagged.

"It kinda sounded like it growled at me," Mech answered back sounding unsure. Mech never sounded like this before. He was always the arrogant bastard, always had something wise-ass to say, but this time he seemed genuinely shaken.

Stick to the plan. That WAS the original plan. But that was before they discovered that the main building appeared to be completely abandoned in the middle of the day. That was before the unanswered phone calls. And the closest thing they got to talking with someone other than fellow crew members of the Atlas II, were from a couple of growling things. Toller decided it was a good time to deviate from the original plan. Sometimes you just gotta wing it.

**

On the way out they saw something move from one of the office cubicles. A couple of the overhead fluorescent lights flickered off and on and it made a buzzing noise as it did so. They approached the desk slowly with Ketan leading the way, muffled noises coming from right behind one of the walls, and the sound of things being knocked about. He motioned for Toller and Ingrid to stay back and to mute their com-line temporarily. They were completely unarmed. Astronauts don't usually come packed and loaded, but most of them have been trained in hand-to-hand combat, a skill that had proved to be completely useless so far until possibly now. Ketan grabbed a desk lamp, yanking the cord off the wall socket. Height-wise he was above average, 6'4", clocking in at about 215 lbs. during last weigh in. He had never been in a real physical fight in his adult life, just as an elementary schoolboy. Even then he was at the receiving end of the beat downs. Crouched down, he approached the cubicle where the noise originated from. All of a sudden he was very aware of his heightened senses. His heart felt as if it was trying to pound out of his chest. He breathed through his mouth like a panting dog trying to cool off. The buzzing of the flickering fluorescent light was amplified tenfold. His palms were sweaty and cold. He turned the corner at the opening of the cubicle and froze.

"What's going on?" Toller asked as he approached Ketan.

The lamp slipped out of Ketan's grip as he stumbled back. He recognized who was in front of him at first glance. It was Dave, the office clerk that everyone liked because he was funny as hell and he told the raunchiest dirty jokes. He was also handicapped and got around with the use of his wheelchair. Only this Dave didn't look very human at all. His skin had the appearance of a lightly charred fabric. There were areas on his arms and face where there was no skin at all. You can see the muscle and caky, crumbling dried blood. It looked like there were algae growing on parts of him. He must have weighed a fraction of what he used to be. His face or what resembled his face had an emaciated look. His lips, paper-thin and cracked and revealing too much of his pale gray gums and stained teeth with bits and pieces of stringy meat stuck in between. Dave's facial expression is unnaturally contorted, with glazed eyes that revealed nothing. His once full head of hair now only had a few patches left. And that god-awful smell, it was partly coming from him. Ketan had only smelled something comparable to that once a long time ago. It was during a city-wide strike, back when he was twelve years old. The trash didn't get picked up for two weeks. The entire neighborhood stank like fresh from the shitter sewage had just exploded out into the surface. Ketan remembered his father setting their pile of trash on fire to rid of it. He assisted in the whole operation unfortunately and saw a crapload of maggots writhe and curl as he tossed a lit match on the garbage heap. He remembered catching a good whiff of it all and puking all over the sidewalk. This smell was worse than that.

"Geez, fuck, what the hell...what happened to you Dave?" Ketan struggled to get the words out of his mouth. Just as Toller had turned the corner, Dave let out a primal scream as he suddenly moved his wheelchair forward, throwing his full weight upwards and propelling himself midair as he headed right towards Ketan's abdomen with his decaying mouth open, bare teeth and festering tongue in good view. It missed but caught Ketan's forearm through his jumpsuit, tearing away skin and muscle from the crook of his elbow down towards the wrist. The thing's shoulder hit the partition wall then landed belly down still chewing on the piece of flesh. A bloody piece of fabric dangled from the corner of its mouth.

Ketan stumbled back and tripped on Toller in the process. Ingrid came from behind and rushed towards the thing (which was now flopping face down on the floor) with an unscrewed wooden mop handle and started to beat on its head. It seemed unaffected, as it crawled and pulled its way towards Ketan's feet, following the trail of blood gushing down his right hand. Ingrid turned her attention back to her comrades, Toller already holding Ketan up on one side. She hooked her arm around Ketan's waist then altogether they hobbled as fast as they could towards the exit. The thing let out a growl similar to what Toller had heard from earlier.

The three of them stumbled out into the great expanse of the base lot, the sun already partly down, dimming everything into a gray wash. They could still hear the thing groan and grunt from inside.

Ingrid was the first to notice.

There were people coming out from the support buildings.

She could only see silhouettes from where they stood but there was something peculiar about their movements. She couldn't figure it out but something about it made her not want to call out to them. She turned to Toller who was now just noticing the activity.

She was about to tell him something when from a distance she heard a growl, followed by another one. They all started to make that noise. They just kept coming out of the buildings and they all grunted and made that god-awful noise.

And they were all headed for the shuttlecraft.

Toller flipped back his com-line to normal status and alerted the crew back in Atlas II.

"Mech, grab the essentials and get the crew outta there, now!"

"Cap, I've been trying to get a hold of you for the last ten minutes, what the fuck just happened?"

"Just do what I fucking tell you and get everyone outta there!"

"Ingrid, stay here, keep pressure on his arm and keep him awake, I'll be right back."

"Captain, where are you going?"

"Getting us a ride."

**

Toller knew exactly what he needed to do and where he needed to go. He went towards the hangar situated right behind the main building.

The first goal was to get his crew out of here.

The second was to find out what happened nine months ago.

For now, the prime directive is survival.

He took a military grade vehicle large enough for his crew and grabbed some artillery on the way out.

A million different things went through his head as he drove back.

He saw Natalie, Mech and the others huddled around Ingrid and Ketan.

And the things - they were now past the shuttlecraft and were headed towards them.

Natalie approached him as he jumped out of the vehicle and quickly noticed the guns strapped to the shoulder holsters.

"Captain...you're armed, what's going on?"

"I'm not sure but it's not safe here. Let's load everyone up."

With that, she helped the crew get on board the truck, with her sitting shotgun upfront. Toller reached into a compartment down the middle, pulled a gun out and handed it over to his first officer.

"If any of those things come near you, shoot 'em."

She hasn't held a firearm since training but she was very capable of using it. It felt strange in her hands, cold and menacing. She laid it flat on her lap.

Toller looked back towards the back at his crew like a protective father making sure that his kids had their seatbelts strapped.

Then he quickly glanced at his side view mirror. Those things moved quicker than they seemed earlier now that they were closer. That guttural growl was all he could hear as they took turns like it was some kind of call to others. This was how they communicated. His hands gripped the steering wheel tighter, feeling the tension going all the way up to his arms and shoulders.

The truck sped past the main building and around the hangar from which he took the vehicle and artillery. Something caught his eye on his way past the building where Mission Control operated from. A digital ticker had been installed by the side of the wall. It must've been put up after they left, he didn't remember having it around prior to. A scrolling text went from right to left. And as he read what it said, chills ran through his body.

The message: To the flight crew of Atlas II, Welcome Home!

He stepped on the accelerator pedal and sped past the main gate which was unsurprisingly left unguarded and open.

The growling noise faded as they drove further away from the base.

Captain Toller Lee and his crew once again treaded the unknown as the setting sun gave way to darkness.

Chapter 1: Sleep My Darlings

October 2020

The children slept soundly in their room, a rare occurrence this early in the evening. Just a few hours ago they spent a good chunk of their afternoon playing out in the rain. It was heavier than a drizzle but lighter than a downpour. The clouds hung low but didn't appear ominous. It was a soft kind of sprinkle, the type that was perfect for naps, reading a book, watching movies at home, or letting little children experience playing out in the rain for the first time.

The five-year-old twins had their nuclear yellow raincoats on with the matching clunky boots that made them look almost cartoon-like. They ran after each other and took turns going in and out of the plastic playhouse and maneuvering around the swing set playscape in the middle of the yard. Their mother sat out on the front deck, just a stone's throw away from where the kids were. About an hour ago her phone made a cheery little noise alerting her to a newly received text message. *Got out early, on the way home. Luv you.*

**

Cormac had just looped the chain up twice on the gate at the entrance of their home. He had plans of eventually getting a remote gate hooked up but that would have to wait. For now this will do. He jumped back into his white SUV and drove slowly down the unpaved driveway which curved in a serpentine pattern. The drive up to the house was lovely during the daylight hours but somewhat creepy during those late nights when he'd left the office way past business hours. He'd volunteered for extra shifts at work to help cover for unexpected expenses at home. He'd been looking forward to the three day weekend. Finally some time to hang out with the wife, the twins, the two dogs and all the cats who've adopted them as their family in the last decade. What he really looked forward to was having time to work on his manuscript. He was about halfway through his novel when Helena got pregnant with the twins and he had been slowly plugging away at it piece by piece since.

The gravel road opened up to a clearing and he spotted the kids from a distance with their yellow outfits on being ushered up the deck by their mother. He honked his horn a couple of times as he swung around to the left and parked the truck underneath the carport. He flipped his jacket collar up, put his baseball cap on and ran towards the house with briefcase in tow where he was greeted by the kids who grabbed a hold of his legs. Helena took the briefcase from him, stood on tippy toes and gave him a quick kiss.

"You let them play out in the rain?" Cormac asked as he dragged one leg after another, the twins giggled as they held on for the ride.

Helena gave him that *Don't be so uptight and let them be kids* kinda look. "They had fun. We don't get snow out here, this is all they have. Besides, they had raincoats on the whole time."

"This is supposed to be a bad storm. I don't want them getting caught out here with flash floods."

"There are no flash flood warnings in this area. You really think I'd put my babies in danger?"

You mean, OUR babies. Cormac let that last sentence go. No need to nit-pick every little thing. He's already got a headache, no need to add on to that with a squabble.

They all stood in the mudroom. Cormac hung his jacket and baseball cap up on the wall brackets. "They're gonna catch a cold or something." The kids hopped off his legs and took their coats off. They sat on the bench and waited for mom to help them pry off the mud-spattered galoshes from their tiny little feet.

"Mac, they're in kindergarten. They go to school with a bunch of snot-nosed ankle biters, they are gonna get sick. They'll be fine. Quit worrying so much."

He hated it when she called him Mac. He'd told her time and time again not to call him that. So when she used it in that context, he was fully aware that it was being used to push his buttons.

Helena had the kids fed and in their flannel jammies in no time. She was a good mother to the twins but her parenting style was much too relaxed, a complete opposite of how Cormac was. He was raised in a strict household with rigid rules and set routines. There was no room for spontaneity. This got him in a lot of trouble as a young man. He spent a lot of time locked in his room reading and later on as he grew older, writing. It was his means of escape. He'd written his first stories when he was only a few years older than the twins. He'd been very vocal about wanting to be a writer as a teenager which was quickly discouraged by both parents. His father had been a mechanic all his life and he wanted at least one of his three sons to pick up the trade and join him in the family business. His mother was a school nurse for a while and never thought much about artistic pursuits.

Most of Cormac's spare time was spent at the local library, even landing a job there as he put himself through college. His younger brother, Tom, took after their father's interest in automotive repair and eventually became a partner in the garage. Toller, his older brother focused on his science degree and never looked back. Cormac finished college with a diploma in creative writing and by then had married his high school sweetheart. The first two years of his postcollegiate career was spent teaching literature and creative writing to high school students in the city. He only worked a few hours during the day which left him plenty of time to take on freelance work as well as work on his own projects. One of which was a novel. Helena worked as an executive chef then. Their careers were their life. Somehow, the schedule and the pace worked for them.

The day he found out that Helena was not only pregnant but was carrying twins, everything changed. Their tiny studio apartment was not fit for a family of four plus pets. Helena would have to stay home with the kids, at least until they were a little older. He had to hustle and he had to get them out of the city. It was then that his writing projects were temporarily put on hold and he took on a job upstate at a marketing firm. He'd found a large house with several acres of land that needed work which made the price tag very reasonable. It was an hour away from where he worked but the price was right, it had a beautiful view of the hills and it was nothing like living in the city. He'd put in quite a bit of work and money into fixing up the place slowly. Between the babies and the renovations, their savings was just about tapped out. Finances have been tight but they've always managed to stay afloat somehow. The pressure on him had been tremendous, a pair of hands around his neck slowly tightened its grip. Fortunately, he was the type who thrived under these conditions. Determined to pick up where he'd left off with his writing, he secured a couple of freelancing gigs which was a boost to the old bruised ego but what's been eating him inside was his unfinished book. For the past month or so, he managed to carve in a little bit of time to devote to his manuscript. A paragraph here and there but nothing monumental.

**

Helena had cooked up a pretty good spread followed immediately by a fresh pot of coffee. She knew how much Cormac had been itching to write and she wanted to give him space. She was good to him that way and he appreciated it.

"You're the best, you know that?" He told her as he walked towards the den. "I promise, tomorrow, we'll spend some time together."

He stopped by the third room to the left to check up on the kids. Surrounded by stuffed toys, heads rested on fluffy pillows, he gave them both a kiss on the forehead and made his way to his den.

Helena spent the rest of the evening huddled on the couch with a book. She enjoyed her times of solitude but deep down missed the fast paced work as a chef. She would have preferred if Cormac just watched a movie with her that evening but she was just glad to not have him in one of his foul moods.

He'd been steadily growing irritable by the day, she noticed. This started about a few months ago. He'd taken up to drinking more when at home, usually within the confines of the home office. He never liked to drink where the children could see. She figured that the stress from working such long hours was the main reason for the changes but she wasn't completely convinced of the fact. She was too afraid to even ask. Once, he'd gone into a yelling rampage. She had to put the kids to bed early with the television on and the volume turned up just so they wouldn't hear their father's belligerent rants. He blamed her for losing his momentum with his writing. If it weren't for her carelessness they wouldn't be buried in debt and he wouldn't have to be working so damn hard and he'd surely be a published author by now.

Cormac never really saw himself ever having children. She knew that. He once said that he was too selfish to be a parent. He wanted to travel the world and do as he wished in his own time and you couldn't very well do that with kids in the picture. Even so, Cormac adored his family. His tendency to be overprotective of the kids stemmed from his upbringing, which she understood. They've been together long enough now for her to realize that sometimes all he needed was space.

Cormac stared at a blank screen in his den. He'd been sitting there for the last 15 minutes sipping his coffee. He used to be able to weave words effortlessly but these days he had to have a running start to get the rusty old gears going again. Over to his left were a stack of papers - his partial manuscript. He flipped through the pages and read random passages in an attempt to get his mind focused on this sole task. That was his greatest challenge these days, his inability to keep his mind on one thing. He struggled to get the words out of his brain. With eyes closed, he envisioned himself amidst the story, walked in the characters' shoes, spoke with their tongues then slowly he rebuilt his inner world one word at a time as he continued to write all the way past midnight.

Afterwards, Cormac set his laptop aside, made his way towards the living room where he found his wife curled up on the couch, the book she was reading had fallen open face down on the floor. He crawled up next to her and wrapped his limbs around her body. She reciprocated by pushing up closer to him. His thoughts drifted away and his body experienced an involuntary spasm, a slight twitch, an indication of relaxation. For the first time in what seemed like a long while he felt content. That night, his dreams brought him to places he hasn't visited in ages, once again a voyager in the realm of fantastic and wondrous things. There he remained until late in the morning.

**

He woke up to find his wife shaking him violently, her hands grabbed on to his shoulders. She was in tears and in a panic. Cormac sat up, groggy. He held on to Helena's forearms to keep her steady.

"Hey, what's wrong?"

"The twins..." she sobbed in between words. "They're not waking up."

"What do you mean, not waking up?" Cormac got up and stumbled-ran towards the twin's room, Helena trailed right behind her.

"They're both usually up by now for their Saturday cartoons, so I tried waking them up and they just wouldn't."

Cormac approached Allen first. He sat by his bedside and gently shook the child whose cheeks were red and flushed, Cormac relieved that his initial thoughts were wrong. He felt for the child's pulse, strong and steady. He did the same for Alice. Same results. Both the children appeared to be alive and healthy, but in a state of some deep slumber. Cormac swept Alice up in his arms hoping that it would stir her up enough to come out of it, but the child just slept on through. Her body remained still in his arms, her little limbs dangled by the sides like a rag doll.

Helena sat next to Allen and kissed his forehead, her tears dripped down on a tuft of dark hair.

"What's going on here, Cormac?" She wiped her face with her sleeve and cradled the boy.

"I don't know." He usually had the answers. Whether it was a fact or just flat out bullshit. He always had an answer for everything. He drew a blank with this one. He was always referred to as a fountain of knowledge. Sure, he knew plenty about everything but with no real expertise on the subjects. A dilettante. A big fat phony.

Helena had her cellphone out and was dialing a number in desperation. "I'm calling 911, we just can't sit here and not do anything."

"No don't do that, what are you gonna tell them? The kids are sleeping soundly and not waking up? You know how silly that sounds?"

"That's exactly what I'm gonna say. You got any better ideas?"

"Yes, actually I do. Call Toller."

The operator on the other side of the phone had already picked up:

"Please state the nature of your emergency. Hello? 911, please state the nature of your..."

Helena hung up and looked at Cormac with a stunned expression on her face.

"You haven't spoken to him in ages."

"I know. This is different. He's a smart guy, smarter than I will ever be. The man is on a groundbreaking mission somewhere up there. If anyone's got answers, he should."

Helena called the number that Toller had e-mailed them. It was a gateway number that patched them through the ground control interface especially built for communications for family members and loved ones only. They had to have a passkey, and an approved phone line to bypass security. The process usually took a couple of minutes to connect from caller to recipient. Not bad for getting in touch with someone currently not even on this planet.

**

Capt. Toller Lee was in the middle of working on a weekly status report for the entire operation - a herculean task that he dreaded to do but could not delegate to another officer. It was his sole responsibility to gather all accumulated data from all the main operations, interpret it in a somewhat comprehensible form and send it back to the powers that be down below. It took a lot of money to keep this type of rig afloat and those who were in charge of the fundraising had to continuously show proof that it was not all for naught.

Toller snickered to himself as he thought about the entire procedure. "I'm an astronaut for hire." He shook his head. "Send me to space and I'll track you down some extraterrestrials."

He had always been the sarcastic cynic. The sarcasm was a coping mechanism. The cynic part, it was something he picked up from his father. As with Cormac, the pressure was on him, even more so as the eldest, to join his dad in the garage. He was a hopeful candidate due to his aptitude for picking up things rather quickly. He was always good with mechanical things. As a kid he took apart his toys, including his bicycle, analyzed the parts, and then put it back together. It gave him a greater understanding of how things worked. His young logic dictated that if he knew how things operated, then he knew how to control it. Control would give him power and in his rebellious mind, powerful people were desired and envied. To be young and stupid even with all that intelligence. In retrospect, it all made sense at the time. The older he got, the more he saw past all that. The veil had been lifted and he saw the world for what it was. He had earned his place in this ship, seen the Earth from an outsider's perspective, walked on moons and defied gravity, and yet, in a simplified state he was just a marionette with invisible strings controlling his every move. Strings that could be cut off at any time if they chose to do so. Scientific advancement or not, if THEY decided that this mission or any other future ones did not warrant all the money that was spent on it then it was over. Just like that. Then it's curtains to you Captain Lee. You would have to settle for a job at a research facility or maybe even teach. Those who do, do. Those who can't...

His thoughts interrupted by his personal com-line going off alerting him to a call. It startled him. Nobody ever called besides his now ex-wife. This better not be her. He saw the number and recognized it immediately. He only sent out a handful of passkeys. Each crew member had to submit at least three people that they wanted to be able to get in touch with them while they were away for this mission. It was a mandatory policy. The counselor assigned to the crew felt that it was important to stay connected to those they've left behind. Living in isolation could cause depression, anxiety and prohibited productivity. So the obvious solution was to stay in touch.

He picked up the call, unsure of what to say. "Hello. This is Toller."

"Toller, it's Helena, Cormac told me to call you."

The sound of her voice indicated that this wasn't your ordinary greetings and good tidings type of call. This can't be good. "What's wrong?"

Helena had already handed the phone over to Cormac. "Toller, it's me. Something strange is going on with the kids. I didn't know who else to call. I hope I'm not bothering you."

"No, not at all, what's wrong with the twins?" An uncomfortable long pause followed the question.

"They went to bed early last night and now they won't wake up from their sleep."

"What do you mean? Are they breathing? You should call for help."

"Yes, they're breathing, they look to be perfectly fine, just not able to wake up. And I am calling for help. That's why I'm talking to you."

"Mac, I can't do anything from out here, you should take them to a hospital."

"Do you know of any condition similar to this, there must be a medical explanation, right? We always used to read those books about weird scientific facts, remember? The ones with the really tall people, the ones that could hold their breath under water for hours, the ones that only slept for an hour a day."

"Yeah, I remember, but Mac this is different. You should get them checked out."

"I will, I just needed to talk to you first. I know you have things you need to do but if you can try to find out something for me, please."

"I will. Get a doctor to come over your place, I'll see what I can find out and I'll call you back."

"Thanks Toller, I appreciate it."

"Send my regards to Helena, take care of yourself Macky."

**

Toller had heard of something similar happening before. It was an extremely rare disorder which caused the affected to sleep on for hours, days, and for the very few, even weeks. For both the twins to experience it was a deviation in itself. For it to happen simultaneously was bordering strange. He saved his status report for later, left his quarters and headed towards the main cabin to seek the expertise of his crew.

As he turned the corner he bumped into Ketan who looked uncharacteristically shaken.

"Captain, I was just on my way to see you." He fidgeted while he spoke and he rubbed the tips of his thumb and index finger together, a nervous tick.

"What's up K? You look a little distressed."

"No offense Cap, but so do you. Anyway, I just got a call from my sister, you remember me telling you that she moved back in with my mom to help her with running the apartments?"

"Uh-huh, she's the one in the East Coast right?"

"Yeah, her. So she called me just a few minutes ago saying that she can't get mom to wake up."

Toller tried to keep his cool but he squinted his eyes when he heard this bit. That usually happened when he was trying to analyze something.

"Cap, that's not all, it gets weirder. Right after I hang up from that call, I get another one from my other sister. She was in a panic, said she's been trying to wake my nephew up for an hour but he just kept sleeping. I mean, they're alive and everything, just asleep." Ketan became conscious of his fidgeting and stuffed his hands down his jumper pockets to try to control it. "So what do you think it is?"

"Funny, I was just on my way to ask you the same thing. I just got a call from my brother. My niece and nephew aren't waking up either." It was disconcerting for Toller to see his Science Officer reduced to a bundle of nerves. The only thing he could think of doing was to talk to the rest of the crew and go from there.

Toller led the way and Ketan followed right behind him. He went up a flight of stairs and through a maze of narrow hallways which converged into a larger opening. The sensor was tripped and the door opened for them as they entered the main cabin where the rest of the crew was already huddled together, some of them still in lounge clothes. They all looked up in unison as they sighted the captain. Ingrid spoke first.

"Captain, we all just received some disturbing news back home."

"Let me take a wild guess. Your loved ones aren't waking up from their sleep." Toller scanned his crew members' faces as he uttered those words. The look of surprise and confusion, crinkled foreheads and all, washed over them. It was like watching a stadium crowd do the wave.

"Ingrid, patch me through Mission Control. We need to find out what's going on."

Mech was already fiddling with one of the touch screen com-lines scanning for info. "Captain,

I think you should see this." He swung the screen around and pointed at live data streaming in,

"I just set up an RSS feed of similar cases being reported and in less than a minute, there's been over a hundred results and counting." Mech could be a complete knucklehead at times but when it came to gathering info, data, stats, and hacking into authorized-only sites, he was the one you wanted on your side. "I can map all the locations out for you if you want."

"Yeah, do that." Toller swiveled the screen back towards Mech as he looked up to the main screen. Ingrid had just established visual-com with CTX Mission Control and Toller was now face to face with Carl Mendelson.

"Capt. Lee, what a pleasant surprise, this unplanned meeting. You're getting more spontaneous in your old age."

"I'm not here to shoot the shit with you Carl, what in the hell is going on down there? And don't tell me you haven't heard about it either."

"Your guess is as good as mine Toller. I've already sent half my people home due to family emergencies. We're working at half capacity here and we're making it work. We expect the same from you guys up there."

"Keep us updated with any developments."

"I will Toller. Take care."

Toller looked at Ingrid, "Are we off-line?"

"Yes, Captain, both audio and video transmission has ended."

"Good. That useless son of a bitch. He knows something and he's not telling us. I can feel it."

"Hey Cap, you're not gonna send us to our quarters and tell us to get some rest are you? Because there ain't no way I'm getting any sleep now," Mech hollered from across the room. Always the smart-ass.

"No, only if you want to. But if you're gonna stay up, someone better make a giant pot of coffee and start digging out some info since we're not getting any straight answers."

Before Toller could make his exit, Mech had something else to show him. "One more thing. Got that geo-data for you. I'll link it to the main screen so everyone could see."

"You read my mind, go for it."

A map of the North American continent flickered on the main screen. Red dots indicated similar occurrences as it was reported. A new red dot flickered every second all throughout the nation.

"Back it up just a bit Mech. I wanna see the whole thing."

"You got it, sir." Mech zoomed out to include a worldwide view of the map. Just as Toller suspected, the red dots cropped up everywhere. It wasn't just local.

This thing was spreading all throughout the world and at that very moment, nobody knew how it started, how it spread and how to cure it and how to prevent it. What made it worse was that they were all up in space, completely clueless. Spectators from afar and there was nothing they could do but watch, wait and stay awake.

Chapter 2: All Fun and Games

"Die! You evil zombie motherfucker!" The reanimated corpse burst into flames and burnt into a crisp as Randall lit him up with the flamethrower. He was testing out the new game he ordered online using his old man's credit card. He was expecting another shipment today - a couple of POV shooter games, and an extra controller for his girlfriend for when she comes over shortly. Randall had a severe case of Senioritis. An affliction that hits most 17 year olds in their last year of high school. He managed to coast for the last three years and he was not about to change the formula now. He'd been playing hooky for close to a week. Usually his old man would've been all over his case for skipping school but his daddy had been sick and sleeping for the last four days. That only meant one thing to Randall. His bruises would finally have time to heal. A little bit of freedom before the beast awakened.

The fact was, his old man never got sick. He had been in construction all his life and he was as fit as a gladiator. So when he missed a couple of days of work, Randall knew he went down pretty hard. He really didn't give a shit what happened, he was going to leave after graduation anyways. He planned on joining the army or something. Anything. Anything to get away from Doyle.

Randall's mother died giving birth to him. And old man Doyle had been giving him hell ever since. Randall even tried running away a few times but the cops would just bring him right back. There was really no rhyme or reason to how Doyle operated. He just liked picking on the boy.

One time Doyle made Randall watch as he fucked one of his regular floozies. He remembered it well. He felt the old man's big hands grab the back of his neck as he directed him towards the room. "Grab yourself a couple of beers boy."

Randall walked towards the mini-fridge and took out a couple of cans of cheap domestic brews. Doyle snatched one of the cans from Randall and shoved him down on the recliner. Doyle pulled the tab open, the popping noise gave way to the fizzy foam of booze. "This is better than a birthday cake son. Today I'm gonna show you how to be a man."

Those television shrinks would assume that Randall would have been ruined by that and they would have been dead wrong. Sure, there was no doubt of its long lasting effects on an impressionable child's psyche. He learned to cope with it. What choice did he have? That was all in the past now. You gotta deal with the past and let it go or it'll catch up to you. It helped to think of the things that made him feel good: his best gal (Samantha), his hound dog (Winger), and driving.

Winger jumped down from the couch and ran towards the door and sat perfectly still. She let out an impatient whimper.

"What a good girl you are. Is your Sam here?" Randall patted her head and opened the door. Sure enough Sam was walking up towards the house. Winger bolted past Randall's leg and ran towards Sam, jumping up and licking on her hands.

"Hi babe." She gave Randall a quick kiss on the side of his mouth and walked in. "Are you all packed?" She tossed her backpack off to the side and plopped down the couch. Winger followed suit and rested her head on Sam's lap.

"Been packed since last night. You hungry?"

"I can eat."

"Good, made us some pancakes. Already ate mine."

Randall walked off to the kitchen and grabbed the plate he'd made for her out of the microwave.

"Awww, look at you cooking me breakfast. That's sweet."

"Yeah, yeah. Just trying to do somethin' nice. Scoot over."

Sam and Randall had been planning this camping trip for a while now. It just never came to be. Old man Doyle has a vintage Airstream camper that he used for hunting with his boys. Now that he'd fallen ill, Randall thought it was a good time to take it for a weekend joyride.

"You sure this is a good idea?" Sam said before she shoved another mouthful of syrupy flapjacks, saving a piece for Winger.

"Of course, it's gonna be fun camping out with my two favorite girls."

"You know what I mean. Your dad's gonna be royally pissed when he finds out we borrowed his camper."

"Sam, he's barely moved since he caught that flu. I doubt he's gonna remember anything this past week. Just drop it, ok?"

"What about all this rain?"

"What about it? The campsite's open. I called to check. We live out in the hill country. It hardly ever floods here. Are you done worrying?"

"I can't help it. I've been watching too much news lately. Have you seen the weather reports? They're calling this an unprecedented event."

"A little bit of rain and everyone freaks out. I just don't get it. Anyways, we should head out in a few."

Randall made his old man a peanut butter sandwich and left it by his bedside along with a pitcher of water.

Outside, Sam and Winger were already in the truck getting comfy for the road trip. Sam tweaked the stereo settings and settled for the first classic rock station she could find. Winger sat on a blanket in the back seat chewing on a new squeaky toy.

Randall hopped in the truck already guzzling down his second can of energy drink. He switched gears and the engine rumbled into a steady hum as it pulled the silver bullet of a trailer with ease. They had the weekend all to themselves and life was good, at least for the moment. Randall drove in a leisurely pace, enjoying the Texas landscape that stretched out in front: a combination of lush rolling hills and flat fields and wide open skies that made you want to chase the edge of the horizon.

**

Doyle sat upright in the dark room, chest heaving like a cat about to cough up a hairball. He gripped the edge of the mattress and threw his head back gasping for air. Something's not right and he knew it. His guts hurt from deep within and he wanted nothing more than to eliminate it. No stranger to extreme pain, he was a pro at this by now.

A nail gun incident at work had his left hand stuck on a frame until the medic pried him off of it. A motorcycle spill sent him sliding across gravel at

40 mph, peeling the skin right off during contact and by the time he'd slowed down from the impact, parts of his body looked like tenderized meat with burnt leather stuck to it.

But whatever this was he was feeling, was beyond the scope of any pain he had ever felt in the past. Just then he felt his abdomen push up, he clutched his arms around his midsection and fell on his knees. He vomited bile and mucus at first, followed by thickened blood and bits of dark meat. He gasped for air in between and continued to expel dark matter, as if his insides were put through a blender. This went on for what seemed like an hour but in all actuality, only ten minutes had gone past.

The pain was gone now as Doyle wiped his mouth and chin with his sleeves. Now that the sensation of excruciating pain was gone and over, it was replaced by a ravenous hunger. A craving. For what, he wasn't quite sure but he stumbled to the kitchen to look for something.

He caught a glimpse of himself on the full-length mirror on the back of the door. What he saw was someone he didn't recognize. Sunken eyes with enlarged pupils that stared back at him. His pale skin almost had a grayish-green tone under the surface, like growing mold. A week's worth of facial hair covered the bottom half of his jaw. Thin, cracked lips hid pale gums and blood-tinged teeth.

Back to the food. His thoughts snapped him back to his main task. His only concern at the moment was to find something to eat. Never mind the cold chills he felt throughout his body. Had he taken his temperature at that moment, he would have realized it was way below the normal limits. Never mind the fact that he'd soiled and pissed himself on the way to the fridge. That wasn't important. What mattered was nourishment. He searched the fridge for something that would trigger his senses. He found leftover rotisserie chicken and took several bites of it in hopes that it would satisfy his craving. It had no taste whatsoever. Everything he tasted was bland and made him nauseated. He came across a pack of sausages in the back of the fridge and tore the cellophane open. The smell of raw meat triggered his salivary glands which caused him to drool excessively. He dug his fingers into the casing and shoved handfuls of raw meat into his mouth. This was closer to what he'd been craving but it still wasn't quite what he looked for. This would have to do for now. The first bite reduced the hunger pangs inside his abdomen into a dull ache. He sat there on the linoleum floor with his back against the open fridge feasting on his find when the doorbell buzzed.

The delivery man held a medium brown package addressed to a Randall Woods. It required a delivery confirmation otherwise he would've just left the darn thing on the porch. He rang the bell a couple more times and started to fill the slip so that the recipient could pick it up at the post office.

Ben hated this job, hated the uniform and despised his boss but it was all he could do to keep his old lady from kicking him out.

Doyle headed towards the living room without a care for his appearance. He was aware that he wasn't the same person as before and was fine with it. All he cared for was to keep the pain at bay.

Something outside smelled awfully good and he was drawn to it. He opened the door and saw a man standing there with a box. The man appeared to have a faded, washed-out blue tint to him. Yet another change to adjust to. Everything Doyle saw was desaturated and lacked true colors.

"I've got a package for Randall Woods, please sign over here," Ben handed over the scanner to Doyle just as he looked up and saw the state of the man in front of him. "Geez, are you alright? You don't look so good."

In his head, Doyle said something like, "Yeah, I'm fine, just very hungry," but what actually came out was something resembling gibberish. A grunt, at most.

What stood in front of him stimulated Doyle's salivary glands again, even more so than the uncooked sausages he had just consumed. Thick mucus dripped from his slightly-parted lips as he lunged forward taking a bite out of Ben's left shoulder.

Ben screamed and he stumbled backwards as this stranger right on top of him sank his teeth in deeper. Ben managed to kick him off and hobbled his way back to the delivery truck.

Doyle chewed and sucked on the small piece of flesh he was able to tear off. He was aware that this was an unacceptable behavior but that voice in his head was overtaken by the taste and flavor that filled his renewed palate. He was disgusted and satiated all at once. He wanted to say, "Goddamn, this is the most delicious thing I've ever tasted," but what came out was unintelligible rubbish. A low growl. He licked his fingers clean and sucked on his nails to get every bit of flavor out. He felt full but still wanted a second helping. Doyle was sorry to see the delivery truck speed uncontrollably past the driveway heading towards the end of the street and disappear from view altogether. He thought about chasing him but his pick-up truck wasn't there which could only mean that the boy had taken it for a ride. He felt no anger. Just hunger and a slight pain. He retreated back in the house, curled back into bed and waited for his son to come home.

Chapter 3: Running the Red

"Goddammit all to hell!" The delivery truck swerved from one side of the road to the other barely missing a mail box. Ben steered with his left hand which freed his right one to apply pressure on his injured shoulder. "This ain't worth ten bucks an hour."

He took a sharp turn on a winding road and nearly tipped the truck over along with the rest of the day's packages still stacked in the back. The pain was not only unbearable but had also caused a partial loss of feeling on his left arm. He had no choice but to switch hands on the steering which left his wound to bleed freely. He reached the intersection and had just missed the light. It was the longest red light he'd ever stopped for. Logic dictated that he return the delivery truck to the depot, pick up his ride and drive himself to the

Elmont Medical Center and get this bleeding mess of a wound on his shoulder patched up. But all logic went out the window when a customer sank his dirty teeth into him and pulled a piece of his flesh off. So fuck logic.

Left turn lane was the route to the depot. Right turn lane would take him home. The light turned green and Ben cut off a minivan and got himself on the right lane. He felt lightheaded, cold, and hungry. He could see the apartment building from here, just one traffic light away. He would not miss it this time. Ben ran the red and was shortly pulling up to an open parking space. He stumbled out of the truck and up three flights of stairs. Alli should still be home, she usually didn't leave until an hour from now. He rang the bell, leaned on the door and waited. "Alli! It's me, lemme in."

He buzzed the bell one more time and kept his finger on the button this time.

"Babe! Open the damn door, hurry!" Still no answer.

Ben fiddled with the keys and managed to let himself in.

"Alli, where the fuck are you?" Ben grabbed the half empty bottle of vodka off the bar and guzzled a few good gulps down. It burned his throat going down and tasted nothing like the way it was supposed to. He poured some on his wound the way he'd seen in movies which proved to be a bad move. "Aaaaaahhhhrrgghhh, fuck!"

He walked into the bathroom just as Alli stepped out of the shower, startled from all the screaming.

"Shit, babe, you're bleeding!" She wrapped a towel around her torso. "What the fuck happened to you? Shouldn't you be at work?"

"People shouldn't be biting other people either but we can't have it all can we?" Ben sat on the toilet, leaned back and took another swig.

"Huh? What are you talking about?" Alli dug around the medicine cabinet for something to clean the wound with.

"You heard what I said. Some guy bit me babe," Ben answered.

Allison gave him a puzzled look. "Why the hell would he do that?"

"I don't know, I didn't stop to ask, now will you please just get me a bandage for this thing?"

"You really should go to the hospital, all we have is some gauze, some wrap and some cream."

"That'll have to do. Just fix me up."

"Get in the shower first. You have blood all over you."

Ben stripped down and let the warm water rinse off the metallic blood smell that covered most of his left side. The initial contact hurt worse than the actual bite but it slowed down the bleeding a little. Allison wrapped his shoulder up post-shower.

"You really need to go to a hospital. I think that could be infected. It's probably a good idea to file a police report too. This guy sounds like he's not playing with a full deck."

"No! I'm not going anywhere. I don't have insurance and I'm not paying all that money for a couple of bandaids. I just wanna stay home and eat. I'm really hungry baby. Can you fix me up something?" Ben popped down a couple of pain meds and parked himself on the couch.

"I need to leave for work in a minute. Speaking of, I'm gonna have to borrow your car tonight, mine's got a broken tail light. I don't really wanna get a ticket. We barely have enough money for groceries as it is."

"I don't have my car."

"What do you mean? How'd you get home?"

"I drove the delivery truck home, didn't want to stop anywhere."

"What?! You gotta call you work and tell them what happened. They're gonna want their truck back."

"Fuck them and their packages! I'm not sure if you noticed but I'm fucking injured here. I think that's more important than that stupid job."

"You mean you still have packages in there? You've gotta be fucking kidding me Ben. You need this job. We need this job."

"Of course, I still have packages in there. What, you expected me to deliver those things, bloody shoulder and all? Come on, where's your head? And thank you for your concern by the way."

"Ben, we need this job, it took you long enough to find this one after you quit the last one. You promised me."

"Damn it, Alli. I really don't need this right now. Just once I want you to be there for me. Now get me some food, I'm fucking starving."

"Be there for you? Be there for you? I've been there for you. I'm working my ass off to pay bills while you drink it all away." She packed her duffle bag with the usual arsenal. Outfits, makeup, perfume. "I'm going to work. You do what you want to do. Make your own food. I'll see you when I get home." She slammed the door on the way out and left Ben to fend for himself.

Ben got up and hobbled towards the balcony. He opened the sliding glass door and stepped out in his robe. Allison had just started her car up, broken tail light and all. She pulled out of the carport and sped past the corner.

"Wait! You can't just leave me here like this! I need you Alli! Allison!"

She was already gone.

Ben finished off the rest of the vodka, hurled the bottle out and watched it break into tiny little specks of glass on the lot. He hobbled back inside and slid the door shut. The throbbing pain on his shoulder resumed as his hunger intensified into a savage craving. He wasn't sure which pained him more. This hunger overpowered his senses and was now audible. The gurgling noises from within demanded to be fed. His sides ached more than his actual injury which now itched around the edges. First things first. Some food. He went straight for the fridge to scout. Nothing in there smelled right to him. He went for the freezer where he found some frozen chicken with bone in. Something told him that this would have to do for now. Ben clawed into the packages and sank his teeth into the frozen meat. He gnawed and trashed his head about to bite through it but nothing worked. He just couldn't sink his teeth in through all that ice. Desperate and famished, he ran hot water through the frozen meat to soften it up. He drooled in anticipation as his feast defrosted. It was then he came up with the idea. It'll have to wait until after dinner. He tore through the meat and sucked on the bones. It didn't make sense to like the taste this much but it silenced the craving. The smell of uncooked poultry initially revolted him but the taste was unlike anything he had ever tasted.

Alli once took him out to a steak house for his birthday. He ordered a 14-ounce prime rib medium rare. It was cooked to perfection and had just the right balance of lean meat and fat. It melted like butter in his mouth. The best meal of his life. This was way better than that. The only bad thing about it was that there wasn't enough of it around. Somehow, he had to get his hands on some more raw meat. This was good but it had to be fresher. But first, he had to follow through with his idea.

He went into the hallway closet and got out his toolbox. He pulled out a file he used to saw off plumbing pipes from his previous job. Ben hobbled into the bathroom and switched the overhead lights back on. The face in the mirror was not his. It was washed out and pale. Grease from the chicken he consumed smeared his mouth. Ben pulled his bottom lip down and inspected his teeth. He did the same with his upper lip.

"This just won't do anymore," he said. Only it was actually more of a groan. With his mouth wide open, he took the file and started to sharpen one tooth at a time. The first tooth was rough since he didn't have the space to wedge the saw into. Each tooth carved into a razor sharp point.

"Better to chew with," he told himself.

His gums bled. His lips cut and bruised. He managed to get the bottom front row done. Pleased with his handiwork but tired from the effort he retired into the bedroom. Under the covers he shivered and rested. He planned on going to the store to get more meat. Ben ran his tongue over his newly sharpened and jagged row of teeth and cut his tongue in the process. The phone beside him rang a few times before the voicemail picked up. Shortly after, his cellphone rang from the other room. It was still in his pants.

"It's gotta be my work," he muttered. Ben picked up the phone and dialed the number to retrieve the message. It took him a minute to remember the code.

"Hey Ben, this is Kenny. Call me ASAP, need to know your location. Your shift was over an hour ago and the truck never made it back to the depot. I'll try your cell. This is very urgent."

Ben threw the phone across the room and pulled the covers up to his neck. He had the chills and the hunger had subsided to a low rumble for now. His body stiffened and ached, Ben felt the change within. It felt like a virus swept through him, with all the symptoms occurring in rapid succession. He felt like shit, his thoughts were foggy and the only thing that made him feel good throughout this entire ordeal was the consumption of raw meat.

**

Alli pulled up to the back of the club. She dug deep in her purse and fished out a brand new pack of menthol lights. She tore the plastic off it and pulled a stick out. She placed it between her lips and reached down the drink holder for her lighter. She flicked the lighter and watched the flame dance as she drew it closer to the tip of her cigarette. She let the flame go and took the stick out of her mouth and placed it back into the pack.

"I can't do this." She placed her hands on her belly. "Not anymore."

She looked up and stared at the dull exterior of the back building in comparison to its flashy neon bedazzled front complete with red carpet and faux marble lion statues that flanked the entrance. The dark side of the moon. "I won't be doing this for long either, I promise." Alli grabbed her bags, walked past the bouncer and into the club.

**

Back home, Ben had fallen asleep with thoughts of feeding. Feverish dreams of madness filled his head with images of the past. Familiar and forgotten faces faded in and out. A picturesque view of the house he grew up in crinkled and folded from the center outwards as if on fire. Scenes played out through an old film reel blemished with antiquated marks, scratches and cigarette burns. Then black ink seeped in through the sides and flowed into the frame, fanning out into vein-like formations. It weaved a complex net of black mesh which corroded everything in its path. This surreal trip down memory lane reached a dead end. A black pool of nothingness.

Ben jolted from sleep with a gut-wrenching pain at his mid-section. His chest heaved as he gasped for air. Blood dripped from his upper lip where he bit through with his sharpened lower teeth. The bite wound burned and itched like hell.

He tore the bandage off his shoulder in one swift motion which revealed a throbbing infected layer of tissue covered in blisters. He hacked and vomited bits of bile and dark matter. A violent episode followed by an intense craving. A craving that spoke to him in a loud and forceful voice. It only knew one word: FEED.

Chapter 4: Sick

"Turn it up, I like this song," Randall said followed by a long last drag of his cigarette. He flicked it out the window just as the song was interrupted by static and the beeps of an emergency broadcast system. The message came through choppy as they drove through the low parts of the hills.

"Ah, coooommee ooonn," Randall screamed at the car stereo's direction as if it had intentionally interrupted his song. "It figures."

"Wait, I think it said 'this is not a test' this time." Sam fiddled with the stereo settings. "Probably another thunderstorm warning."

Randall looked out and up at the sky and noticed nothing out of the ordinary. "Ok, maybe it's not a thunderstorm."

"It's breaking up, we're at the bottom of the hill, can you speed up just a bit?"

"You don't have to tell me twice to speed up."

They reached the top of the hill where the radio signal came through loud and clear.

Beep. Beep. Beep. This is not a test. A nationwide advisory has been issued to stay home until further notice due to a widespread report of a rare condition that causes severe lethargy and chronic sleepiness. This message is by the emergency broadcast system. For more information, contact your local authorities. This is not a test. Beep. Beep. Beep.

Sam turned to Randall. "Babe, your dad."

"What about that asshole?"

"Nothing. I just thought you might want to go home and check up on him or something."

"Why would I want to do that? He's a big boy. The man of the house. He'll manage without me."

"What about you? Maybe you should see a doctor, if that thing is contagious you might've caught it."

"I feel fine. Just drop it alright? I've planned this weekend forever. Don't ruin it."

"Fine."

"Fine."

"I'm just saying."

"Look, we're here." Randall pointed out to the state park sign sandwiched by a couple of boulders.

**

With the camper fully hooked up, Randall started up the portable grill while Sam got the fire going. Winger ran around the fire pit stopping every so often to bark at the flames. They lucked out on the location and being off-season, there weren't that many people out there. They passed by several other campers on the way in to their site. Up ahead, the smoke from another fire pit was visible.

It was a quiet spot over all, just the faint noise of kids goofing off. Typical of this time of the year, it got dark earlier than usual and along with it came the temperature drop.

"Steak's almost ready, hope you're hungry."

"I'm starving. Need another beer?"

Randall guzzled down the rest of his bottle. "I do now."

After dinner they sat on foldout chairs by the fire and drank. Winger was not too far off enjoying her piece of steak.

"Why didn't we do this sooner?" Sam asked as she hooked her arm around Randall's.

"Would have been hard to do without a truck and a camper." Randall stared at the firepit as the flames flickered and danced.

"You still wanna get a place together after graduation?"

"Yeah, I think we should. We'll save on bills and I need someone to take care of my sorry ass." Randall nudged Sam.

"Only if you're a good boy."

Winger had finished her steak and was now flinging the bone around.

Sam sparked up a cigarette. "You're not going through with that military thing are you?"

"Probably not. I won't last a day there with my attitude. Me and authority figures just don't mix. Maybe I'll stay local. Get a part-time job and sign up for classes at the junior college." Randall guided Sam's hand towards his mouth and took a drag out of her smoke.

"Ditto. Sounds like a good plan."

Winger sat in front of them and whimpered. Sam reached down and scratched her ear. "Of course, my little Winger's coming too." Winger lay down afterwards and let out a big sigh.

"Not to be a Debbie downer but I'm just worried..."

"About what?"

"When your dad finds out we took his truck and his camper."

"I'll deal with that when it happens. I get in trouble for things I haven't even done yet so it doesn't matter much what I do. Does it? I've learned not to worry unless there's something to worry about."

"Makes sense. Sorry. No worries until there's something to worry about. I like that."

"Cool. Getting chilly out here. Ready to go inside?" Randall looked around and stuffed his hands in his jacket pockets.

Winger ran up to the entrance of the camper, looked at the door and looked back at her people.

"Winger wants in, so I guess I'm voted out. Was starting to freeze my ass out anyway. Is the generator gonna hold up for the night?" Sam asked.

"Got plenty of juice for the weekend, don't worry."

They left the fire burning outside as they hurried in.

**

Winger growled at something outside. Sam, a light sleeper, got up and took a piss. She scratched the top of Winger's head to settle her down.

"What's the matter, hun? You smell a raccoon outside?" Sam parted the blinds to peek out.

The blazing flames in the fire pit were now reduced to scattered embers. It was quite dark outside, even with the moon right above them. She thought she saw something crouched by the grill. She squinted her eyes to focus on it and saw movement.

"Babe, wake up, wake up. I think I saw something outside." She shook Randall to stir him.

"Huh? We're out in the middle of nowhere. Probably just a raccoon or something. Get back in bed." He pulled the covers halfway up his head.

"No, it was bigger than a raccoon, what if it's something else? Winger's really bothered by it."

"Winger's bothered by everyone she doesn't know."

Just then a series of loud banging noise came from the rear of the camper.

That got Randall's attention. "What was that?"

"I told you there's something out there!"

Randall put his clothes on and reached for something in the overhead cabin right above the foldout bed.

"Where'd you get that gun?" Sam asked.

"The old man got it for himself last Christmas."

"Is it loaded?"

"What good is a gun with no shells? Besides, this is old man Doyle's gun. So, yes. It's loaded. I'm going out. Stay here."

"No way, I'm going with. In case you need back up." Sam dug into her backpack and pulled out a rolled up canvas cloth. She'd unrolled it to reveal a medium-size camping ax.

"Where'd you get that?" Randall asked.

"It's mine. What did you think I have in my pack, make up and an evening dress?"

"Well, no."

"Are we going out or what?"

Randall switched on the exterior light that flooded one side of the camper with an ethereal bluish glow. The banging noise continued, undisturbed by the illumination. They emerged from the camper cautiously. Randall was first out the door, Sam right behind him with Winger trailing.

"Whoever's here, I just want to let you know we're armed so this is your chance to get lost. You go your way and we go ours, let's just forget this ever happened. You just woke me up from a good sleep and I'm not in the mood for this shit."

No response. The banging continued. The foldout chairs were strewn about. The grill appeared untouched. The rolling cooler, however, was ransacked. They walked towards it.

"Ah shit, I forgot the cooler outside. It had all the meat in there. It's probably a raccoon or a possum that crawled up in the storage area back there and got stuck."

The cooler was upside down, packages of meat torn open, its contents long gone. "I'm just gonna have to run down the hill tomorrow and get a few things from the store. What a waste. I can't believe I did that." Randall shook his head in frustration.

He set the gun down on the ground by his side as he picked up the cooler to turn it right side up. He could hear Winger still growling at something. Sam was midway between him and the camper.

"That sounds too big to be a raccoon," Sam said as she looked towards the silver Airstream.

Just then, Randall shut the cooler's lid and on top of it were handprints. Bloody human handprints.

A growl from behind. Sam screamed, "Randall, watch out!" Winger barked non-stop. It all happened so fast.

Out of nowhere this thing charged up towards Randall and knocked him down on his back. All he saw was a blur. Randall managed to grab the gun before he fell and used it to keep the man at an arm's distance. "Get off of me or I'll shoot!" Randall couldn't see his face because of the lighting from behind. Just a shadow figure of a thin man. Sam, with ax in one hand, grabbed this man by his collar and yanked to try getting him off of Randall. The man turned around, distracted, his attention solely on her. Sam got a full view of the attacker and was in shock.

Randall, now upright, fired a warning shot overhead then aimed it at the man who was now closing up on Sam. "Leave her alone!!!"

Nothing but a growl came out from the attacker. He just stood there rocking back and forth, stepping uncomfortably closer towards Sam each time. Winger stood next to Sam, growling and barking at the attacker. The man looked at Winger and licked his lips with its bluish-black tongue.

Sam still frozen in shock, almost mesmerized by what stood in front of her. She saw the face of a savage. Its mouth encrusted with dry blood and saliva. Its lips covered with blisters. Stained teeth and bruised gum exposed as it clenched its jaws and grimaced as if to show: 'This right here, is what I'm gonna eat you up with.' She'll never forget the look in its eyes. A blank stare, no glimmer of humanity left in there. Just a rabid, hungry, animal out on a prowl.

The man slowly hunched down and sneered at her. She could see the saliva dribbling from the corners of his mouth. A blister on his upper lip bubbled up and burst. Mustard-yellow liquid oozed out and dripped into his mouth past his teeth. He hunched down until he was almost crouched. He bared his teeth one more time and with no warning he let out a primal growl and jumped towards Sam.

Sam snapped out of it and did the first thing that came to mind. She grabbed her ax with both hands by the handle, brought it up and over her head, then with her weight behind it, flung it forward. She ran off to the side.

All Randall saw was the man lunging towards Sam. "Sam, move away I'm gonna shoot!" He first fired a shot aimed at his leg. The man fell forward. Sam ran towards Randall as he approached the fallen man.

"Don't touch him, he's not right."

"You're goddamned right, he's not normal. He just tried to hurt you. I need to make sure..." Randall flipped him over with the barrel of the gun and his foot. He had an ax half-buried in the middle of his forehead.

"His face..."

"He tried to bite me."

"He what?!"

"He tried to bite me. I think he was hungry."

"Why would anybody do that?"

"I told you, I think he was hungry. Look at his face, his teeth. He ate all of the meat in the cooler, Randall. Raw meat. Guess that wasn't enough."

Randall cocked and aimed the barrel at the man's chest. "I think he's dead." The man on the ground looked at both of them, sneered and flaunted his teeth. In one swift movement it somehow got himself upright and in a crouching position again. Sam, Randall, and even Winger backed up a few paces almost in unison.

"Randall, shoot him. He's about to pounce."

"He should be dead."

"Randall, shoot him!"

It lunged forward.

"Shoot him!!!"

Randall steadied himself, held his breath and pulled the trigger.

The bullet hit the thing's head. Dead center.

It split the head almost all the way down the middle. A large chunk of it came flying off. Blood and brain bits splattered the side of the Airstream.

Sam walked over to the edge of the camper. Her ax. She had to retrieve it. It was still embedded into that thing's skull. She stepped on the bone, grabbed the ax handle and pulled. It was wedged in there and held solid. She didn't think she had it in her to do that much damage. She pulled harder and pried it loose. She wiped the bottom of her shoe on a patch of grass to get the blood off.

Randall had already lit up a cigarette. He held the gun across his chest as he took long, deep drags of his smoke. He was visibly shaken as Sam approached him. "Drag?" He asked her.

"Yes, please."

She took a long pull and it tasted good. She held it in for a while then blew it out. The air was crisp and cold. It almost hurt to breathe it in. A rush filled her head suddenly, a light headed feeling took over. "I need to go inside. I have a headache."

"Me too. We need to get out of here."

Randall took his flannel shirt off and wiped the side of the camper off. All it did was smear the blood to a pink tinge. Not completely clean but less visible.

"That'll do for now," Randall said as he entered the camper. He turned off the exterior lights, poured himself a drink and held Sam in his arms as they figured out what just happened outside.

Chapter 5: The Answers You Seek

"This is Dr. Meyers speaking."

"Hello doc, this is Cormac Lee down at Nameless Road. I wouldn't be calling you on your emergency line if this wasn't an emergency..."

"Are you unable to wake Helena up from sleep?"

"No, it's the kids, and how did you know?"

"You haven't seen the news?"

"No, why?"

"The country is in a state of emergency, an outbreak of sorts. People are advised to stay put until the matter is resolved. Typically your best bet would be the medical center but I just got a call from there and was told that they're at full capacity. No one is being admitted until they set up the temp clinics by the east wing."

"Outbreak? What am I supposed to do? I've tried to wake them up. Nothing's working."

"Nobody knows what it is or what caused it. All I know is that it causes severe lethargy and chronic sleepiness. They'll probably come to on their own."

"How long is that?"

A long silence hung in the airwaves.

"Doc?"

"There's a rare sleeping disorder similar to this where affected subjects sleep anywhere between 24 hours to as long as six months."

"How is that even possible?"

"The subjects do get up, eat, relieve themselves but they never come out of the deep sleep state."

"What about this virus? How long do the affected sleep?"

"I wouldn't call it a virus, Cormac. At this moment I'm afraid it's unknown."

"You mean you don't know?"

"Nobody knows."

"I need you to come over and take a look at the kids."

"Cormac, I don't think that will help. It's best to just keep them as comfortable as possible."

"Doc, please, I don't know who else to go to."

"I can't..."

"Doc, remember that favor I did for your son when he just got out of the facility? I put my neck on the line at work to get him a job as a clerk. Remember?"

"Of course."

"And you made me promise not to tell anyone about his problems because it's a small town and word gets around fast."

"It'll be an hour or so. My wife's asleep and I have to get back and take care of her."

"Thank you, thank you. See you then Dr. Meyers."

Helena plugged in a portable space heater and set it at the foot of Alice's bed. She pushed the twin's beds together thinking that it would help keep them warm if they were in close proximity.

Their skin was cold to the touch, and they shivered under their blankets. Helena had placed a plush dragon toy in Alice's arms, her favorite.

"Here," Cormac entered the room with a Chthulu plush toy and handed it to his wife. "This is Allen's favorite. I know it creeps you out but he likes it."

Helena cradled the tentacled toy and sobbed as she kissed it then placed it in Allen's arms. Cormac pulled the covers up and tucked them in.

"Is he coming?" Helena asked as she wiped her tears with her sleeves.

"Yeah, it'll be awhile but he's coming." Cormac picked his nails, a nervous habit.

"He said there's some sort of condition going around." He thought twice about telling her about the nation's emergency status. Besides, he needed to gather more information.

"What kind of condition?" Helena asked.

"He didn't say much, only that it causes sleepiness. I'll ask him more about it when he gets here." He kissed the children on their forehead. At first glance they appeared to be two healthy kids with rosy cheeks in a deep peaceful slumber.

"Sweet dreams my little darlings," he whispered to both.

"You should get some sleep, you look tired." He walked around the bed towards his wife who sat at the edge and stroked her curly hair. She said nothing and crawled under the blanket next to Alice.

"Maybe it's better to sleep in the other room. If this ends up being a virus then it's contagious. I don't need you getting sick too," Cormac said.

"If this is a virus then we probably already have it too. I'm staying with the kids."

"Ok." He hated her stubborn streak. Once she had an idea in her head there was no way to change her mind about it. Right or wrong, she'd go through it.

"What about you?" She looked up and held his hand.

"I'll sleep later. I think I'm gonna dig around online and see if I can find more info while I wait for Dr. Meyers."

She nodded her head, already half asleep.

"Goodnight babe." He kissed her on the cheek and tucked her in.

**

He grabbed a can of energy drink on the way to the living room. He turned the TV on and clicked through channels. All the usual shows appeared to have been interrupted by news. Each channel broadcasted live. He settled on one and turned the volume slightly up. A female journalist was on location in front of the local medical center where it appeared to have some sort of barricade at the entrance of the hospital. A mob of people gathered and huddled. A pre-taped shot from earlier played as the newscaster filled in details. Images of emergency tents erected at the parking lot. Generators being hooked up to provide power to the outdoor clinics. Rows of stretchers ready for patients.

Newscaster: We've been told by sources that the med center is at full capacity. Nobody is allowed in, no exceptions. Not even staff. No one is allowed to leave the premises either. This is all done in order to contain the disease. We just got word that the CDC is on their way to set up camp here. The people are out here wanting to get to their loved ones. However, the temp clinics are set up and currently functioning. They've already admitted 60 more patients since I last spoke with them.

The ticker tape below scrolled: The country is in a state of alert and emergency, please be advised to remain in your home until further notice. The cause of this condition is currently unknown but experts remain diligent in finding answers. The President is scheduled to address the nation in the next hour. Stay tuned for updates.

Newscaster: With no clear answers from the authorities, people are clearly in a state of panic. Not only in our town but across the nation. Here with me is a local resident who's been patiently waiting to be let in the hospital where his wife was admitted last night. Sir, can you tell us more about your situation?

Man: Yeah, my wife's been there since yesterday. They tell me she's in a coma but I know better. It's that sleeping disease they don't want you to know about. Those people in there have no idea what they're dealing with. All I want is to take my wife home. The news says that it's a sleeping disorder. If that's the case then I can take her home while she sleeps this off. They just wanna be able to bill me for a longer stay. That's all it comes down to. Money. Always is.

Newscaster: Do they allow incoming calls? Have you spoken to anyone in there to give you a status report on your wife?

Man: Hell, no. If you call the main number you get the same message. They're trying to contain this thing so until they figure something out we're all shit out of luck. Oh sorry, I didn't mean to curse on TV.

Newscaster: What are your plans for now?

Man: I guess I'm gonna go home, make me some cowboy coffee and stay awake as long as I can. They can't even tell me how this thing started or how it spreads so how do I know I'm not infected? What about you? For all I know you're spreading the disease right now. I'm just afraid if I go to sleep I won't wake up for a while. If I wake up at all.

Newscaster: Thank you for sharing your story and best of luck with you and your wife. This is Brenda Garcia for Channel 4 News, back to you Greg.

**

Cormac took a couple of gulps of his energy drink and searched for news online on his laptop. What he found was just as frustrating as the actual junk being broadcasted live. He scoured the main news sites first. Mostly speculations and no facts. He scrolled down to the comments section to see the discussion. Mostly argumentative paranoid trolls who stirred up thoughts of a conspiracy.

Something caught Cormac's attention. A brief comment by Prkrgrl85.

The answer you seek will reveal itself in the awakening.

If you want to live you'll want to see this.

It was a URL link to a video.

Cormac couldn't resist. He clicked on the link.

Chapter 6: True Nature

Welcome to The Playground.

This place stank of rumors and scandals, addictions and perversions. It provided a much needed haven for those in the fringes, edge of night type of characters. The rejected, unsatisfied, hollow misfits and derelicts gathered here to indulge on their secret fantasies. Just pay cover charge and abide by the cardinal rule: Keep your filthy paws off the ladies. Break the rule and you will quickly find yourself outside of the establishment.

The dancers' entrance led to a poorly lit, narrow hallway. The smell of club air hits you the second you walk in. A combination of cigarette smoke, sweat, a medley of perfumes, and just a hint of buffalo wings. The muffled sound of music audible, the enhanced bass can be felt under your feet. Redefining classy.

The first door to the right led to the men's locker room mostly occupied by bouncers and DJs, occasionally shared with maintenance guys. The door to the left led to the main office that housed the management crew. All three of them. It belonged to the general manager (Nicky), his right hand man (Chad) and the right hand man's assistant (Gil). No one knew exactly what Chad's job title was but he was a permanent face at the joint. It was an unnecessary addition since the general manager could have easily juggled the work load but it was a way to pass the work down to someone else. Gil could have made more cheddar slathering burger buns with special sauce but he was content getting a free peek at topless women and acting like a top-notch wannabe big-shot.

The only person who had any street cred was the actual owner of the club - referred to as Yaro. A 40-something guy who used inheritance money from his parent's tragic death in a car wreck to embark on the business of marketing tits and ass to the people of this lovely town. There was this rumor about him arranging his parent's early demise by rigging the family car. Patrons and staff have only seen him once during an impromptu visit. He tipped well, said very little and exited quickly. The second door to the right led to the dancer's dressing room. It also had a direct door that led to the stages.

At the end of this hallway was a door that opened to the back of the joint next to the bar. Alli peeked her head out to get the lay of the land. The place was dead for a Friday night. Payday Friday at that. A quick scan of the room and she figured there were about less than twenty customers out there. Maybe a couple or so at the VIP room.

"Hey little girl, slow night. Nicky said to send people home." Chad hollered from the bar already milking the company liquor.

"Nicky will have to throw me out if he wants me to go home." Alli's a seasoned pro at back talking. She'd learned early on to have a thick skin in life or might as well just quit the game.

"You paying for those drinks?" She asked Chad who already resumed flirting with the new girl at the counter.

"It's on the house, management don't have to pay." He signaled for a refill on his tequila shots.

Alli walked up behind him. "You ever call me little girl again I will have you bent over this bar and calling me daddy. Understood?"

Alli looked up and smiled at the new girl. "Don't believe anything he says, he's just here to hold Nicky's dick when he pees." Alli headed towards the dressing room to change. She didn't expect Nick to be in there chatting it up with the girls.

"Gonna have to send you home Alli." Nick greeted her with a sendoff.

"Nicky, you know I can't afford to go home, let me at least go a couple of rounds."

"Have you seen it out there, doll? It's dead. You'll be wasting your time."

"Let me worry about that. I'm going up tonight. I need to dance while I still can."

"Suit yourself."

"Besides, I don't want to come home just yet."

"Lover's tiff?"

"Yeah, something like that."

"You can always leave that bum and get with me."

"You know Chad's drinking the bar dry right?"

Nicky stormed out cursing his minion under his breath. Alli changed into one of her outfits. She used to put more effort into this production. She used to carefully plan out the songs and matched it with her clothes. She even had everything choreographed. None of it mattered anymore just as long as the end product had her breasts exposed and her ass grinding. She wanted to quit in a few months anyway. She'd put away a little money at a different bank account. She'd put her hair up high and the makeup went on last. She barely said a word to the other women, an outcast among her peers. The subject of envy by many who worked here because Nicky would always cut her slack and allowed her to talk back to him the way she does. No one else could get away with it but her. Call it a special privilege between ex-lovers.

Alli stepped on to the stage as Slash's intro guitar riffs from Welcome to the Jungle echoed through the speakers. Her alter ego's persona kicked in. Her game face on. She became a different person when she was up here. This was her stage and she took command of it. She was the master of her space and beneath her, were her marionettes. She pulled and tugged on their strings and made them feel what she wanted them to feel, made them think what she wanted them to think. In her head she was somewhere else far away from this dingy shit hole.

Only two songs then I'm gone for the night. Just two songs. She ran towards the pole, jumped and twirled herself around it with her head tilted back. The flashing lights spun into a blur and the faces melted and merged along with it. Her senses overwhelmed by a dizzying pace as she strutted down the runway and worked her little puppets into a frenzy.

**

The hunger washed over him in crashing waves. Sharp pains shot out of his sides and made him curl in agony and discomfort. Still in partial control of his facilities despite his appearance, he grabbed the keys to the truck and headed for the parking lot. His memory failed him as he struggled to start the truck up.

"I know how to do this, I know how to do this," he said to himself. Only it came out as a couple of short grunts and a growl. He managed to start it up and get it moving, hitting and side swiping adjacently parked cars as he pulled out. He was headed toward the grocery store right across the highway. Cars screeched and honked as he drove right across four lanes and over a median. There were a handful of Sleepers wandering the streets, their faces contorted into unnatural expressions. There were many people scurrying about. Some hauled cartloads of food into their cars. Some fueled up at the gas station right next to the store. A few had already turned into looting the local liquor store.

Ben drove up right by the entrance and stopped the car. He left it running as he ran in and headed towards the meat section. He drooled and bared his teeth in anticipation for his next meal. People ran about in all directions and barely noticed the Sleepers in the store. Some filled their baskets with water and canned goods. Some went straight for the beer. Some loaded up toiletries and cereal.

Ben approached the meat section and grabbed the first package he could get, in this case, a pack of London broil. He tore the wrapper off, held the cut of meat in both hands and gnawed through it with his sharpened teeth. It tasted even better than the frozen chicken as expected. It was smooth and savory. The blood from the meat squirted from the corners of his mouth and dripped down his chin. He felt every sinewy muscle with his tongue. He devoured it with methodical consistency. For each portion he ripped off, he chewed a couple of times and swallowed. The few other Sleepers in the store who caught a whiff of Ben's meal found themselves in the same section, tearing open packages of beef, pork, poultry parts and miscellaneous raw meat and consuming it right there.

Ben had a small crowd watching him eat until he turned around and they caught a glimpse of his face and his mouth. Ben decided to grab as many of the packaged meat as he could hold onto before all the other Sleepers ate it. Satisfied with his loot he made his way past the scurrying crowd. He was only bothered once by a security guard who grabbed him on his shoulder. Ben turned around and bit him on the wrist. His jagged teeth sank deep into the man's forearm. He applied a slight twist and jerked his head back which tore off part of the man's skin and muscle. That was the first time Ben tasted human flesh and blood and it tasted even better than the raw beef he just ate. It was warm and gamey. It's what he'd been craving all along.

Outside, his delivery truck was nowhere to be found and so he hobbled all the way back home with food in his arms. His hunger satiated for now, he sat on the kitchen floor next to the food and thought about the next wave of craving that was sure to hit him. The true nature of his hunger was revealed to him. He would have to silence the pain within with human flesh. He was revolted by the thought for only a split-second. The old Ben was about to check out. He curled up on the cold tile floor still riding the high from his last meal. He closed his eyes to sleep as a human for one last time. He would not be greeted with dreams from another life this time. He would wake up as a fully transformed member of the Sleeper kind. No recognition of who he was before. He would have forgotten the people he loved, even those he despised. A lifetime of memories erased as he closed his eyes. No dreams. Just a void.

Chapter 7: As Fast As You Can

"What the hell just happened out there?" Sam finished the smoke with a long last pull.

"I just shot a guy, is what happened." Randall dug through a small caddy storage and pulled out a shoulder holster and a pistol. "I knew he had another one of these stashed here."

"He wasn't a guy. Did you see his face? I mean, he used to be a frail, old man but that thing you shot was something else."

"You know, it figures. All I wanted was a nice weekend out with my girls and what do I get? Some crazy bastard eats up all my food, attacks me, then attacks my girlfriend."

"He didn't just attack me. He wanted to bite me."

"Be serious. Why would he do that?"

"You were there! You saw it. He lunged at me with his mouth open like I was his next meal!"

"Are you telling me that guy's some kind of zombie? Because you're out of your mind."

"Damn it, Randall! He did eat all that raw meat in the cooler. Hell, I like my steak rare but I wouldn't polish off that much raw meat at one time. I'm definitely not going to lunge at a stranger just because I'm hungry."

"Whatever it is we need to get out of here. There's a dead guy outside and I killed him. The cops aren't gonna buy this zombie bullshit."

"It was self-defense."

"I'm sure everyone in this park heard the gunshots. We need to go."

Randall strapped the shoulder holster on and buckled the loaded gun in place. Over it, he put his flannel shirt on and his leather jacket. They stepped outside and locked up the camper.

"Should we move the body?" Sam looked at the headless carcass.

"I'm not touching that thing again. Just leave it. We need to split before the park security gets here."

They hopped on to the black pick-up truck and rolled out of the campsite. As they approached the neighboring camper's parking space they heard a woman scream. Randall slowed the truck down. The screams came from inside a pop-up camper. A woman ran from it with a small child in her arms. She was in hysterics as she ran towards a nearby tent where a man stepped out and rushed towards the woman and the child.

"Oh god, oh god, oh god, what happened? Who did this?" The man sobbed and took his son into his arms. "Where's Gracie?" The man asked his wife.

The wife stood there and shook her head. "I don't know, she's gone."

Randall and Sam could see the blood gushing out of the child's neck. His midsection, a gaping hole where organs should be. Sam gagged at the sight.

The man placed his dead son on the ground and called out for his missing daughter. "Gracie!

Baby! Where are you? Daddy's here! Please Gracie let me know where you are. Oh god, where are you?"

Sam grabbed Randall's arm. "We need to help them."

"We can't. We have to go."

Winger whimpered and cowered in the backseat. The truck slowly accelerated past the gory scene. The parents too distraught to even notice their presence there. Randall glanced at the rear view mirror and saw the man pick up something that looked like a dismembered arm. He said nothing to Sam about what he saw.

"The guy who attacked us. He did that to the kid didn't he?" She looked to him for confirmation.

"Yeah, I'm pretty sure he did." Randall answered without looking at her.

This time he drove past the other campsites without slowing down. The gruesome events of the last hour tattooed in his mind and replayed in vivid detail. He drove all the way out of the park without stopping, turned left towards the highway and ran away from it all.

The drive back was quiet and uneventful. A few cars and truckers took advantage of the clear roads. The cold evening air fogged the windshield and side view mirrors. The sky was far from clear. Clouds hung low and glided across. No stars, just a half-crescent moon that glowed an eerie, unnatural honey amber color that blanketed everything around it in a surreal wash. Thick rows of trees lined both sides of the two-lane road which snaked and twisted through the hills.

"What's the plan?" Sam asked.

"Go back to my place and call the cops."

"They won't believe us."

"They'll have to."

"What are we gonna tell them? Sorry to bother you this late officers. We were out minding our own business in a truck and camper that we didn't have permission to take to begin with and this guy came out of nowhere and ate all our food but that wasn't enough so he tried to eat us. You see, we had no choice but to kill him. Right, that's believable."

"You're not helping one bit, you know what?"

"Just being realistic."

"You got better ideas?"

"Turn around and go back."

"What? What for? That is the dumbest thing..."

"We need to show them what happened. They need to talk to the couple about their kids. This just looks like we're running away. Like we're guilty or something."

"But we ARE running away."

Sam let out an annoyed sigh. "Look, just forget it. It's too late to go back anyways. They've found the body by now."

The fuel gauge indicated the gas to be less than a quarter tank.

"We need to stop for gas."

"We just passed a rest stop sign. Should be right ahead," Sam said.

The truck moved to the right lane and exited on to a rest area. Gas, food and lodging were available here. They pulled into a brightly lit gas station. There were more people getting gassed up than they had expected. Each pump had at least one vehicle filling up. Inside, a group of people waited in line to be checked out.

"Fill it up. I'll go get us something to drink." Randall entered the 24/7 store and went straight for the energy drink section. He grabbed two tall cans of their usual, a bag of barbecue chips and beef jerky for Winger. He got in line to pay for the goods when the guy in front of him turned around. He wore a hunter's camouflage jacket with matching hat.

"Nice trailer you got." Hunter guy motioned his free hand towards the Airstream.

"Thanks," Randall said

"You seen anything funny out there tonight?"

Odd question to ask a stranger, Randall thought.

"Not really, pretty slow night actually." Randall was an excellent bullshitter.

"You hear this shit they're talking about on TV? It's all a big ploy to scare the masses."

The guy in front of hunter man chirped in. "They showed a footage of a lady biting a stranger.

Here's the thing. She kept biting him like she was trying to chew a tough piece of meat. She bit down and shook her head like dogs would when they caught a squirrel or something. I guess the guy's arm was too tough so she grabbed his head and bit his left cheek off."

More people walked in just as this guy described the footage and confirmed what he said then added their own theories into the mix.

Young guy with piercing: "Oh yeah, I saw that on TV too. That was sick!"

Mid-40s clean cut guy in khakis: "It's all hype, like everything else they televise. That video was a hoax. Just some bored kids wanting to make money off idiots."

Old man in thick plaid coat: "Y'all need to get what you need here and go home like it says on TV. There's something sinister going on tonight and there's no sense in speculating about something no one has the answers to yet." He cuts in line. "Lemme have a carton of reds," he said to the clerk.

Outside, Sam leaned on the passenger side door with hands in pockets. Randall caught her gaze. She pointed to her wristwatch.

Randall was stuck inside for another five minutes while the local kooks discussed the news. Just as he got in front of the line, a lady from the back hollered to the clerk and pointed to the TV. "Hey, turn it up, they're showing that video again."

Randall shoved his change in his pocket and looked up.

A rerun of a viewer submitted footage played on the screen. First in normal speed followed by a slowed down version. A news anchor's voice narrated a play by play description of the flashing images. It was undeniably a human attacking another human being with a series of bites. First on the neck. She tugged and pulled as the victim unsuccessfully tried to protect himself. Then the attacker went for the face where she tore off the man's cheek and part of his lower lip.

They replayed the video in its raw state with original audio.

The person holding the camera struggled to keep calm as the attack progressed. It started with a wide angle bird's eye view of a residential street. In front of one house a man loaded a couple of luggage in the back of the van. A couple of people ran down the street. One guy power walked towards the bus stop with a rolling luggage in tow. Out of nowhere, a woman jumped out from behind a fence, approached the man and bit him. The camera zoomed in.

Camera person: Holy shit...She just bit the guy (heavy breathing). Hey!!! Leave him alone.

(Banging on window pane) Hey!!!

Oh god, did you see that? (Talking to unidentified person in room) She just bit his face off. (Heavy breathing)

Video transmission ended.

The old man from earlier patted him on the shoulder. "I told ya she bit 'im."

Randall wasted no time grabbing his paper bag and bolted out of that convenient store.

"About freaking time," Sam said to him as he hopped in the driver side seat.

"Something weird is going down right now." The truck sped back into to highway nearly sideswiping a small sedan. "I just saw the news in there. It had a video of a woman biting some guy's face off."

Sam looked at him with a crinkled forehead. "What would make people do that?"

"Not people. Zombies."

"You can't be serious."

"How else are you gonna explain this, huh?"

"Remember the emergency broadcast from earlier?"

"Yeah, what about it?"

"They said something about a virus."

"If that's the case then old man Doyle must be craving brains right now."

"You shouldn't joke about it Randall."

"It's slightly funny. That guy's been out to get me since I was born. Now he'll want to eat me too."

"Maybe we shouldn't go to your place."

"I can't run away from him forever."

"What if he attacks you?"

"It wouldn't be the first time."

"If he's anything like that guy from the park, he'll go for the kill."

"Then I'll just have to defend myself won't I?"

**

Unable to curb his hunger any longer, Doyle took it upon himself to go out back where the chicken coop was and caught his next meal. The taste of blood and raw meat from earlier lingered in his palette and whet his appetite into a frenzy. He held his catch by the feet, upside down. In one motion he grabbed its head and sank his teeth in to the live game. Blood, meat and feathers filled his mouth as he continued to devour it. A temporary placeholder until a better meal came along. The pain inside subsided almost instantaneously. The fresher the food was the better it made him feel and that's all that mattered. He headed back inside the house almost half through with his meal. His insides felt warm but not quite full yet. If consuming fresh poultry gave him this sensation he could only imagine the possibilities if he climbed up the food chain. The thought consumed him, everything else went south.

Doyle couldn't remember his son's name anymore. He couldn't recall a lot of things. The more he succumbed to the nature of his transformation the more he forgot about his past. All he knew was that hunger caused excruciating pain. Give the hunger what it wants and the pain goes away. He collapsed in the middle of the kitchen, an arm's length from the gutted carcass. He was satiated once again and it made him feel powerful. He felt no hurt, no discomfort. Sprawled on the floor he surrendered to the high.

**

The truck screeched to a stop at the curb. "You got both loaded up?" Randall took the pistol from Sam.

"I'm keeping this one." She held on to the shotgun. "I know what you're gonna say. Just save it. I'm going with you."

"You have to stay and keep the truck running in case we need to get the hell out fast."

"I thought you didn't want to run away."

"I don't, but I don't know what's in there. If I get bit I'll turn into one of them eventually. If that happens, you need to get away with Winger."

"If I hear shots I'm going in after you."

"No! Wait until I get out."

"I swear if you take too long in there I'm going in."

"Keep the headlights off this thing in case there's zombies out here."

Sam switched off the headlights but kept the engine running and the heat turned up.

"This is surreal." Randall leaned back on his chair, took a deep breath and exhaled.

"No shit."

"Ok. I'm going. Lock the doors behind me." He leaned over to kiss her then reached back to pat Winger's head.

"Remember. Aim for the head," Sam said.

"I will."

"And don't miss."

"Anything else?"

"Don't get bit."

**

There were no lights in the front of the house but the faint glow of the kitchen light could be seen from outside. The evening chill had a bite to it and it was eerily quiet. Being out in the country, the sound of chirping crickets often dominated the evening, but not tonight.

Randall approached the house with his pistol drawn. His eyes adjusted to the dark quickly as he scanned the perimeter. There was no telling where old man Doyle was. He didn't notice the dried up dark red splotches on the ground near the house's entryway and smudged all over the door.

He reached for the storm door which creaked as he swung it open. He left the main door unlocked when he left which remained just that as he turned the knob and shouldered the door open. It resisted slightly.

He gripped the gun tighter, cocked it, and held it at chest level with the barrel pointed upwards. The living room looked untouched. He checked the back of the door just in case his dad hid there. Clear. *It always happened that way in the movies*, he thought. *The one time I don't check is when it'll happen.*

He approached down the hallway that led directly to the kitchen. To the right was another hallway that led to the bedrooms and the bathroom. He was about to turn the corner when he heard a scratching noise towards the back of the house. His breathing turned short and ragged.

"Don't get bit. Aim for the head. Don't miss," he whispered and repeated it once more. There was no way to prepare himself for what happened next. He gripped the gun with both hands as he entered the kitchen. The stench hit him first. The smell of death and decomposition and something else. He controlled his gag reflex with a quick hand to his mouth and nose. Crouched on the floor, picking through the remnants of the chicken carcass was Doyle.

"Dad?" Randall felt stupid asking. He knew it was him but not. The man in front of him had grayish green mossy-like skin. Areas of his head where hair should be now had infectious open sores. His face had a gaunt appearance like someone stuck a straw in and sucked a little bit of the air out. His blistered mouth was covered in a crusty brown film.

"Dad, it's me." He subconsciously started to back away from the horror in front of him. Just as well. Doyle was already upright, slightly unsteady, but moving towards him.

"Stop right there! Don't make me shoot you. I swear I will." With both hands on the pistol he pointed the barrel at the head.

Doyle moaned then curled his lips inwards revealing his stained teeth and necrotic gums. He let out a growl that made Randall flinch. The strong odor that escaped through Doyle's mouth was unbearably foul.

"Stay where you are or I'll shoot. I'm not gonna say it again."

Doyle staggered forward as he chomped and gnashed his teeth together. Bile-colored saliva drained down the sides of his mouth as the blisters bubbled and popped. He crouched down and swayed slightly from side to side. Randall's seen this before. The man at the park. Old man Doyle was about to pounce. Doyle propelled himself upwards and forwards with his gaping mouth ready to clinch down onto his prey.

Randall often thought about a moment similar to this where he would get back at his dad for years of emotional and physical abuse. *One day,* he always thought, *you'll get yours.*

Doyle was about to get it alright.

Randall never thought it would go down like this.

It seemed to play out in slow motion.

Doyle charged at him. He steadied his grip, aimed for the head and pulled the trigger.

Chapter 8: Changes

Cormac watched the introductory video posted on the landing page of the site. A young woman who called herself Collette sat in front of a white board with illegible scribbles and diagrams on it. A couple of monitors behind her displayed a screenshot of her site logo. This looked too much like all the other trash being uploaded these days but there was something about her that made him want to hear what she had to say. Maybe it was his own desperation.

She showed footage from a local news channel in which a woman bit a pedestrian's face right off his head. She referred to them as Sleepers and likened them to zombies. The idea was so absurd to Cormac that he chuckled when he heard her say the zombie word.

"Pffft, you've gotta be kidding me." He popped the tab open on another can of energy drink and took a quick sip.

Even so, he continued to watch and listen to her talk about the outbreak, the nature of the Sleeper, how to survive the forthcoming onslaught and what the resistance needed to do in order to fight back.

The video zoomed in on her face. She looked directly at the camera as if she spoke directly to Cormac.

"There is no cure. No one is coming to help us. We have to help ourselves. You clicked the link to get here because you needed to know. Now you sit there watching me wondering why should you believe me. My answer to that is in the next video. Right below this one. If you decide not to watch it, then consider yourself dead. If you do watch it, I'll see you on the flipside."

"Arrogant bitch." Cormac didn't realize he said it out loud.

A quick glance at the video below showed him a still frame of a middle-aged woman in a frumpy night gown strapped down to a table. He couldn't help himself. The curiosity would have taken him over faster than this mystery disease could have.

He pushed play.

The camera was situated in an angle closer to the female subject's feet. A slight elevation gave it a perfect view of the woman from head to toe. No narration. Just raw footage.

The test subject wiggled her torso as she pulled and tugged on the restraints that kept her wrists bound to her sides. A simple combination of three zip ties around the wrists and a thick nylon rope looped through it which was then pulled down, tucked underneath the bed frame then looped around and across the body several times before being tied into knots. Across her chest was a thick bright orange strap similar to those used by movers to lift large pieces of furniture. It was looped twice over and clasped to the side of the wooden bed frame. It did a solid job of keeping the shoulders pinned down. The same set-up was used to bind her legs down. One positioned a couple of inches above the knees and another midway between her knees and ankles. Her ankles were bound by the zip tie and nylon rope contraption which was pulled straight down at the foot of the bed and then tied into a knot onto the frame. Cormac noticed an open sore on the woman's left leg.

A complex network of simple restraints which rendered the subject almost completely immobile and stiff on her back. Her head was left without restriction which enabled the woman to lift and pivot her head.

The subject flailed, kicked and wriggled despite it. She opened her mouth to speak but only a grunt emerged, followed by a series of groans. She had a pallid complexion with splotches of greenish blue blemish throughout. She stopped struggling for a few moments only to make way to a series of abdominal contractions. The woman appeared to be gasping for air when a gush of dark fluid spewed from her mouth and dribbled down to her cheeks, her chin and some even into her nostril. An expulsion of what looked like an oil slick and unidentified bits continued. She lifted her head as she growled and spit towards the camera. The gurgling noise from its throat quieted down. The vomiting ceased and the subject was motionless. Seconds later, the subject raised her head and looked towards the camera. Her focus set on someone unseen as her gaze followed someone towards the foot of the bed. Footsteps could be heard and some other unidentified background shuffling of objects.

Cormac leaned forward sensing that something was about to happen. He hovered the cursor on the video's timeline. It only had another five minutes left give or take.

The camera shook and shifted as Collette positioned herself in front of the shot.

"This woman behind me was bitten less than eight hours ago by a child infected by the disease. Right here, on her leg." She pointed at the same sore that Cormac had noticed.

"She fell ill with flu-like symptoms shortly thereafter. Within half an hour of the bite she fell into a deep sleep. She went into a coma-like state which allowed me to apply these restraints on her uninterrupted. What you just saw was her turning into a Sleeper. They get bitten, they sleep, and when they wake up they vomit their insides out just like what you saw her do. After that is when they have cravings. The hunger takes over and becomes their directive. At this state consider them dead and dangerous. They may look like your husband, your wife, your lover, you mother, your father, your child, but all of that's gone. As far as I can tell they retain residual memories. They sort of remember faces and places but nothing more. Stay away from Sleepers. Their hunger can only be satiated by raw meat and fresh blood. Their pain can only be relieved after they've consumed their meal. We just got bumped off the top of the food chain. The only way to end this is extermination. This woman behind me, growling and clawing to get out..." Collette motioned towards the woman.

"Eight hours ago she was my mother. Now she's a Sleeper." She walked over towards the head of the bed raised her right arm and aimed a small handgun at the woman's head. The woman raised her head in anticipation and licked her lower lip. Her mouth covered with newly formed blisters. Mucus-like strands dripped from the corners of her mouth as she snapped her head towards Collette's arm. A click then a shot rang.

Cormac flinched in his chair, covering his mouth with his left hand to keep from screaming, knocking over his near empty energy drink in the process.

Collette walked three paces and faced the camera. "What you saw was real. It's happening in our town. Maybe the entire nation. Even the world. All of you out there watching this...you don't have to believe me. I just shot a Sleeper that used to be my mother. She was the last of my family. So yeah..." She trailed off in her thoughts and looked down as she struggled to hold back tears. She sniffled and wiped her eyes dry with her hoodie's sleeve, gun still in hand. As she reached towards the back of the camera to turn it off, the image of a dead human turned zombie and blood splattered white wall delivered a gut-punching reality to the last 48 hours in the Lee household.

There were three more videos uploaded since he started watching. He was about to play the next one when the doorbell rang. It took him a second to remember about the home visit. He shut the laptop closed then sprinted towards the door. He turned the lock clockwise which unlatched the bolt. He swung the right side of the double door open and as expected Dr. Meyers stood right outside.

"Thanks so much for coming Dr. Meyers," Cormac stepped aside and led him inside his home.

Dr. Meyers was a short, stocky man in his late 50s with a full head of silver hair slicked back with greasy hair product. His glasses sat on the bridge of a prominent nose accentuated with a well-trimmed full beard. He had beady eyes that framed his bushy old man eyebrows. The man looked like a cartoon character as he rushed into the house with a backpack slung on his right shoulder. He carried with him a white doctor's jacket.

Cormac shut and locked the door behind him and wasted no time leading Dr. Meyers into the children's bedroom. Helena was already up and pacing by the bed. Dr. Meyers entered the room not saying a word to Helena, just nodded in her direction. He walked towards Allen's side first and set his backpack down. He put on his white doctor's jacket with his name embroidered on it as if the visit wasn't official until he had the costume on.

"How long have they been asleep?" He pulled out a stethoscope from his bag and put it on as he tilted his head down, looked above the rim and alternately glanced at Cormac then Helena waiting for a response.

"Umm, almost a couple of days now, give or take," Cormac replied.

Dr. Meyers leaned over the boy, placed the chest piece on his torso and moved it around at several spots. He walked over to the other side of the bed and did the same to Alice. Afterwards he placed his stethoscope around his neck and stuffed his hands in his pockets.

"Their heart rate had significantly slowed down. In fact, it's barely audible."

Helena sank into the rocking chair and sobbed.

Dr. Meyers took a penlight out of his pocket, parted Alice's left eyelid with one hand and shined the light with the other. "Same as Luci," he muttered to himself.

"What do you mean same as Luci?" Cormac's patience was already in short supply, between the stress and lack of sleep and now the lone doctor in town appeared to be doing a half-hearted examination of his two very ill children.

"Lucinda, my wife." Dr. Meyers placed the stethoscope back in the bag and zipped it up. "She has the condition too. Displaying the same symptoms. If I took your children's temperature right now I bet it's well below the normal limits of a living healthy human. In case you were wondering why I didn't take their temps, that is."

"Wait, what? Quit the cryptic verbiage and just tell us straight up what you think this is." Cormac advanced even closer to the doctor.

"Mac..." Helena grabbed his arm and pulled on it. "Please, your temper."

"Fuck my temper! I just want some answers. How about it doc?"

"Truth is, I have no idea what your children have. Whatever it is it's the same thing my wife has and so do the rest of the dozen or so people I saw yesterday before I closed up shop at the clinic as advised by my colleagues," Dr. Meyers stated, unaffected by Cormac's display of hostility towards him.

"What the hell kind of a doctor are you? Do your colleagues know something that the general population doesn't?"

"I've told you everything I know earlier on the phone. Last time I got a hold of someone at the CDC I was told to advise my patients to contain the outbreak since they have no known origin for it at the moment and currently no cure. Everything else I know, I got from television reports and emergency alerts."

"Mac, what's he talking about? What emergency alert?" Helena asked.

"I didn't tell you earlier because I didn't want you to worry any more than you already were."

"What the hell is going on Mac?"

"The nation's in a state of emergency. This disease that's spreading causes severe lethargy and chronic sleepiness."

"The government strongly advises the public to stay home until they figure something out. There's really nothing anybody can do. They're in a state of deep sleep right now and it's not advisable to interrupt it. It's like being in a coma, but not," Dr. Meyers added.

Cormac shot him a glare. *You asshole, no wonder your kid turned to booze,* he thought.

"Why didn't you tell me this earlier?" Helena asked.

"I told you babe. I didn't want you to worry."

"I think it's best for me to go now. Just keep the kids comfortable and the second they wake up give me a call."

"Stay right there. You're not going anywhere until you tell me everything." Cormac shut the bedroom door.

"Mac, we can't keep him here."

"Listen to your wife Cormac. This is absurd. You can't keep me hostage here. My wife's at home sick and I need to get back to her before..."

"Before what?" Cormac's eyes widened. He turned to Helena. "You see! He's not telling us everything. Before what, doc?"

"Allen?" Helena pointed at her son whose eyes fluttered open and adjusted to the light in the room.

The little boy's chest heaved repeatedly as he sat up. Dark, thickened liquid spewed out of his mouth and all over his striped pajamas. Seeing their son vomit such volume and consistency startled both Helena and Cormac and kept them frozen where they stood.

"I must warn you..." Dr. Meyers addressed both as he stepped a few paces away from the bed.

"It's only gonna get worse. It's very important that we..."

That was all that Cormac can handle. He grabbed the doctor by his jacket collar and pulled him so close that he got a good whiff of his breath.

"You've been drinking haven't you?" Cormac asked.

"Let me go!"

"What's happening to my kids? Tell me or I swear I'll strangle you with your own stethoscope." Cormac felt pounding on his temples and the blood rushed into his head. "TELL ME!!!"

"They're hungry." The sweat beads rolled down the doctor's forehead.

"Of course, they're fucking hungry, they haven't eaten in two days! I want an answer!" Cormac drew his right arm back, his fist clenched and ready to pounce.

"They hunger for raw meat. Please don't hit me."

Cormac let him go. "Why would they want raw meat? What kind of condition is this? What can we do?"

"You're not understanding this fully. They'll want human flesh. This thing they have. It turns them into cannibals. The disease takes over as they sleep. It's the incubation time. They wake up when it matures. By then, they've turned. There's nothing we can do. There's nothing I can do. My wife...she's sick...I need to get home."

Cormac heard the words but it didn't quite register at first. It only took a few seconds for all of it to add up. "Sleepers," he muttered to himself.

"No, no, no. This isn't happening." Helena's eyes looked crazed and distant.

Dr. Meyer's reached for his backpack by the bed. "We need to contain the children in this room immediately before..."

They've all been too busy dealing with the truth in their own little ways that they didn't notice little Allen lean forward and bite down on Dr. Meyer's forearm.

"Aaaaaaaargh!" Dr. Meyers swung his right arm around so fast that it threw the boy off the bed and on the floor. Blood seeped in through the white coat in a small splotch that quickly turned into a larger one. Allen fell on his side and latched on to the doctor's left leg with his already bloody teeth. This time he locked his jaw as he pulled and tugged.

"Allen, no!" Cormac grabbed Allen by the waist to pull him away from the doctor.

Helena's screams could be heard in the background. Just then, Alice sat up and vomited black matter.

Cormac finally managed to pry his son off the bleeding doctor by leaning back and putting all of his weight into it. He lost his footing and landed on his back. Allen fell to his right with a mouthful of fleshy bits that used to be attached to the doctor's leg. The boy was focused on his first meal as a Sleeper.

From where he was, Cormac saw Helena approach Alice who had just finished expelling the putrid mess. She now looked at her mother and salivated. Cormac got himself up just in time to run over and pull Helena back right before Alice snapped her head towards her mother. He dragged his wife right outside the room and was about to shut the door when the doctor rushed past them and headed towards the front door.

Allen ran towards his father with his mouth wide open as Alice hopped off the bed. Cormac had to think fast. He slammed the door, grabbed the closest chair and hooked it up underneath the door knob to lock it temporarily. He glanced over at Helena who backed up against the hallway wall and fainted. Just as well. It allowed Cormac to grab a bike chain from the junk drawer in the kitchen without worrying if Helena was going to let the kids out. He looped the chain around the door knob and around the chair rails several times and hooked the padlock around it. He could hear both the children clawing and scratching the door. Followed by moans. The door shook.

Please hold. Please hold. He stood on edge as the chain rattled slightly but didn't give way. At that moment he could only think back to the video he saw not too long ago. The video with Collette shooting her mother. He was relieved to see that his makeshift barricade held steady. *There's gotta be a cure,* he thought. Only it was more of a prayer.

Now that the kids were contained in the room he turned his attention to his wife who was slumped over where she had passed out. He scooped her up and brought her into the living room. After laying her down on the couch he noticed the front door open.

The doctor.

He ran towards the door just in time to see the doctor's car turn the corner and disappear from sight. He shut the door, locked the bolt and hooked the chain. Never used the second lock until now. He had installed it when they first moved in just in case. He was used to having multiple locks in the city. Four at one point. It gave him a sense of security. Even a small one. Hard to feel secure when you're harboring those who you're running from.

He walked back towards Helena and checked her breathing and her pulse. Just in case. She seemed fine. Just out of it for now. He covered her up and propped her head up with a bolster pillow. He walked towards the second bookshelf out of the five that filled one wall of their front room. He climbed the ladder and pulled out the fourth book from the left. He reached in between the gap and pulled out a small flask. He returned the book to its place, climbed down, and chugged a few good gulps of scotch. From the other room, he could hear the scratching on the door and the muffled

moans like the monster in his nightmares. Just one
step behind.

Chapter 9: Don't Look Back

She slammed her foot down on her brake as the pick-up truck in front of her screeched into a dead stop.

"Green light means go, asshole!" Alli honked on her horn which was echoed by those behind her car.

A chorus of pissed off commuters just trying to get home in the middle of the night or very early in the morning depending on who you asked. The truck didn't budge. That night she decided to take the back roads home to avoid traffic. She looked forward to a quiet drive. There usually wasn't this many people driving this particular road at this time.

"Oh, come on." Alli tapped her fingers on the steering wheel. Her craving for a cigarette intensified as she grew impatient of the traffic. After the lousy night at the club, barely making enough to cover a week's worth of groceries, she wasn't in the mood for anything but sleep. She wasn't even in the mood for radio. She'd turned the volume down before she left. She'd been dreading coming home to Ben but she hoped that he'd still be asleep and that things would blow over by the morning between the two of them. *Just a bad day is all,* she thought. Even so, she worried about his wound. He would definitely have to get that checked out in the morning.

A quick glance at her rear view mirror. The guy behind her stepped out of his car. Not what she expected to come out of a small sedan. Tall, crew cut, middle-age, glasses, with biceps that can crush an orange. Alli instinctively locked her doors. The man walked right past her car and headed towards the black mid-size truck that blocked the one way lane. Alli thought about driving around but the cops in this area were notorious for being harsh about citations. Zero-tolerance policy for traffic violators. She didn't want to take the chance. She watched as biceps guy knocked on the driver's side window. Nothing happened. He leaned forward to take a closer look into the truck. Alli noticed that all the truck's windows had a very dark tint to it. Biceps guy opened the driver's side door.

"This can't be good." Alli got her cellphone out of her purse, prepared to call the cops in case something went down.

By the time she looked up a woman had attached herself to bicep guy, wrapped her legs around his torso and hooked her arms around his neck as she chomped down on his nose. The guy tried to get her off of him by slamming her back against the truck but all it seemed to do was make her bite down harder. Finally she pulled her head back away from the guy's face. Alli had a clear view of the attack as the guy stood there in shock and reached for the space where his nose used to be. Now it was only a bloody hole of a mess in the middle of his face. The woman tore the nose right off from the bridge and took part of his upper lip with it. The whole time the woman still had her legs around him and shoved the rest of his bloody detached nose into her mouth. She then went after his neck.

Alli watched the whole thing and had forgotten about the phone in her jittery hand. She snapped out of it long enough to dial the emergency number. Two rings and an automated answer. She had been put on hold. The wait time was estimated to be an hour.

"What? What's going on around here?" She looked at her phone, puzzled. She hung up and hit redial hoping to get through. This time around it didn't even ring. She looked at where the guy stood and saw nothing.

A couple of cars behind her drove past and went around the stranded truck. They cleared it just fine with no cops to chase them. Alli shifted her gear to reverse. She was practically sandwiched between two cars and she needed a little bit of room to get around the truck. A hand reached up from outside and below her window. It smeared blood on the glass as it pulled itself up with its other hand. Alli found herself face to face with the attacker that bit the man, separated only by a thin piece of glass. The woman's face was gaunt and grey. Her mouth riddled with blisters. The woman pressed her face up against the window and scratched at the glass. A couple of the blisters popped and secreted a yellowish fluid as she rubbed her face across the glass. Her mouth left a trail of stringy bits of meat and more blood. Then she started banging on the glass. Alli stepped on the gas and nudged the car behind her. She shifted to drive, stepped on the gas and swung her car around, knocking the woman over and clipping the truck in front of her. She heard a small thud as her car lifted slightly. She knew she had just ran over the guy's body but she didn't care. Her car tilted as it hit the edge of the road and went over the ditch.

"Please don't get stuck." She felt the resistance of her tires as it spun in place. It kicked up dirt and dust behind it. The smell of burnt rubber wafted in through her A/C vents. She looked at the rear view mirror and behind the dust that swirled she could make out the figure of a woman running towards her car.

"Come on, come on, come on." She floored the pedal and felt the car jerk forward. She managed to clear the ditch and the truck as her tires screeched on the paved road. She let up on the speed just slightly and looked up her rear view mirror. The woman that chased her just a few seconds ago crouched over the fallen man and clawed her hands into his abdomen, pulling his intestines out and eating it.

Static on the FM stations. A barely audible newscast on the AM frequency was all she could get. She turned the volume up. Alli still couldn't make any sense out of the events that took place. She just saw somebody murdered and eaten. She was almost that woman's next meal. The broadcast came through in spurts. Something about containment and being in danger of vicious attacks. She turned the radio off. She was just around the corner from home. She was eager to tell Ben about her ordeal. *He's never gonna believe it,* she thought. *People just don't bite other people, much less eat them.*

She parked at her usual spot and didn't notice the delivery truck out in the lot.

Maybe he actually did the right thing and drove it back to work. I guess he's feeling better.

She grabbed her purse and didn't bother taking her duffel bag. She locked the car and headed upstairs. The door to their place was slightly open. Ben never left the door ajar. In contrast, he was actually the type that locked everything. She reached into her purse and pulled out a small handgun that she kept with her all of the time. Ever since a customer followed her home one night she was determined to always be prepared. She'd heard too many stories from fellow dancers about the many perils of their chosen work. She wasn't about to be a victim. She used her leg to open the door wider as she reached in and switched on the light with the gun barrel.

"Ben?" She walked into the living room. Nothing looked out of place. Everything just as it was when she left earlier.

She heard shuffling from the apartment above. Not unusual at all, this place had paper thin walls. Their apartment was virtually boxed in by noisy neighbors in varying degrees. Over to the left was Jen. A single mother with three kids from four to seven years old. To the right was a young bachelor who had frequent visitors and made a pass at Alli almost on a daily basis. Upstairs was a young couple who had very loud sex.

Several thuds from upstairs. They're at it again.

Alli made her way towards the kitchen where she thought she heard shuffling when a crashing noise came from above followed by a woman's scream. It wasn't a scream of pleasure this time. She was sure of it. Another scream, only now it sounded more urgent. A few seconds later it was quiet again.

Something was definitely wrong.

Her instinct told her run out, get in the car and go to the nearest precinct. But she heard that noise again coming from the kitchen. It could be Ben. She couldn't just leave him there. She took a couple of steps forward and called out to him again. It was pitch black in the kitchen. She usually had a nightlight plugged in by the sink but it wasn't on this time. The light switch was a few paces away and she would have to step into complete darkness to be able to turn it on.

The terrible smell hit her just as a figure lunged forward. She moved fast enough to dodge and the man landed by her feet. Alli swiftly backed up towards the front door.

"Ben, it's me!"

Ben looked up and clenched his jaws, baring his sharpened teeth in full view. Dried blood and pus covered his mouth. His skin was blue-grey.

"Ben, your teeth. What did you do?" Alli's hands shook as she pointed the gun at him. The smell made her nauseated and it took her a few seconds to realize that it was coming from him. His appearance triggered the image of the woman she escaped from earlier.

She had to think fast as Ben pushed himself up. He looked unsteady and hobbled towards her but she remembered how fast the crazy woman ran.

"Ben, don't make me shoot you. You're sick. We need to take you to the doctor."

Ben let out a low moan and continued to approach her.

If I'm gonna do this, I need to do this fast. No room for error. He's gonna come after me and my baby.

She braced herself and pulled the trigger. Nothing happened. She forgot to cock the gun. Ben was almost an arm's length away as he snapped his head forward, taunting her. She cocked the gun and pulled the trigger again. This time it rang and the bullet hit him on his shoulder. She picked up the wooden stool next to her and flung it at him which knocked him off balance. This was her chance. She spun around and slammed the door behind her as she raced downstairs to her car. Behind her she heard Ben growl from inside the apartment as the door handle rattled.

Don't look back. Just keep running. Get in the car and drive.

She did just that as she hauled ass to her car, got in and locked the doors. Ben was already at the bottom of the staircase when she started her engine. He pointed at her and bared his sharpened teeth encased within his festering mouth. She shifted the gear from park to drive and drove out of there as fast as she could.

Whatever you do, don't look back. Just keep driving.

**

This time she decided to drive on the main road. If she had to pass up another vehicle, she would have more options.

The more options you have, the greater the rate of survival.

A voice from the past echoed in her head from out of nowhere. She hadn't spoken to her dad since she had been with Ben. Now, he was the only thing she could think of. He always talked about being prepared in case of an emergency. This was definitely an emergency and she was headed over to his place. It was just a half an hour away on the outskirts of town. He had a few acres of land and a small house. The house she grew up in and spent most of her time all the way up to the age of 15. She left shortly after her mother passed away. He'd been living there alone ever since. She wasn't too concerned because he cherished being alone anyway. She didn't remember him having too many friends. He'd have company over every so often for a cookout but nothing more. Once, on his birthday, she called but hung up when he answered.

She was a master in avoiding issues in relationships. She had this exterior tough girl act down and most people bought it. Inside, she was a scrambled up mess of denial.

She did send him a card one Christmas.

She didn't have anywhere else to go. Sure, there were other family members nearby but they never bothered to keep in touch with her when things were normal so how could she expect them to act differently now that everything's different. Not even the threat of society itself ending in a cannibalistic outbreak could cure indifference.

She had always been daddy's girl even though he wanted a son. Alli's parents were unable to conceive after she was born. Dad always taught her things. Not just girl-type things. He wanted her to be an independent, strong woman. "No reason you can't be everything you want to be," he used to tell her.

She went through her tomboy phase for a while. She would rather help him fix things up at the house or at the garage. Tinkered with the truck. Patched up fences. That sort of thing. All the way right up till high school. Peer pressure turned the tough girl into an awkward lady. Anything to get a boy's attention. A string of loser boyfriends then followed by a string of even more pathetic guys during the first couple of years in college. Liberal arts course at a junior college was perfect for a girl who had no idea what she wanted to be. Ideal way to procrastinate yet still appear like you gave a shit.

Then Ben came into the picture. She met him at a live drawing class. One that fulfilled an elective requirement. They sat next to each other and cracked jokes about the not-so-attractive models. She was impressed by his natural talent for drawing. He was just happy to have a pretty girl laugh at his jokes. They continued to see each other after the semester ended. He decided to take the next semester off and make some extra cash working at a photo studio closer into the city which meant he'd have to move. He told her he wanted to get a place together and just enjoy life for a while. It was a convincing pitch he gave her. Something about life and love not needing any restraints in order to fully blossom. Bullshit. But she bought it.

Her dad never liked Ben from day one. And Ben knew that. He always brought it up. Always got upset when she'd talk about her father. Always wanted the attention on him. It became another competition for Ben to win. And he did. They both dropped out and never returned. He'd change jobs the way most people changed shirts. His temper increasingly worsened while his drinking habits went along for the ride. She juggled multiple jobs to keep themselves barely afloat until a girl she worked with who had quit came back to show off her brand new sport coupe paid in full with just a couple of months' worth of entertainment. Alli showed up for the audition and was hired on the spot. It took her awhile to get used to baring her tits at anyone who could afford the cover charge. The amount of tips she got made up for all of that. She made good money in a short amount of time and for a little while there, she actually enjoyed her job. Ben didn't want her working there but she paid most if not all of the bills so he had no choice but to just deal with it. Ben was out of a job for nearly a year and it was then that her savings dwindled. Five years later she's burned out, alone, broke and pregnant.

I never should've gone with him.

It only took her five years and a zombie apocalypse to realize this.

**

She drove as fast she can. Way past the speed limit. She figured the cops had more important things to take care of than writing up a speeding car. She was right. All around her, the sound of sirens wailed. From ambulances to fire trucks to cop cars. You name it - it was out tonight. People ran down the streets, some screaming. They ran from those things. Terrible things that wanted to eat them all up. Alarms rang from department stores as people looted booze, electronics, food, prescription drugs, and anything else they could stuff into their pockets or carry in their arms. She was focused on only the road. The rules of traffic no longer applied. There were car wrecks in almost every other street corner. Pile-ups on the highway. Smoking vacant buildings in the distance. A delivery truck engulfed in a blazing inferno right ahead.

Alli was determined to get back home as she weaved through the obstacle course. Death wasn't going to claim her just yet. Not before she had made amends with her father.

She quickly glanced down at her belly, no signs of protrusion yet.

"I'm going to get us home."

Chapter 10: The Inevitable

What's taking him so long? She looked at her watch and saw that it had only been a minute since he went in the house.

A lot can happen in sixty seconds if you think about it. She fidgeted in her seat, kept looking around just to make sure nobody snuck up on the truck. The entire neighborhood looked normal. Nothing was out of place. Just another cold evening out in the country. Except somewhere in those houses, someone's probably turning into a raging cannibal. She felt sorry for those who still haven't heard about the disease. People went to bed thinking they'll get up and head to work, or drop their kids off to school, or go shop for groceries. Instead, they'll wake up to an entirely different world in the morning. That's if they don't get eaten in their sleep. They've been so caught up with everything going on that she didn't even get a chance to check up on her family.

She lived with her older sister who was mostly at work at the call center and only came home to sleep. She'd been her legal guardian since their parents died in a car wreck years ago. The day she left, Missy had signed up to work a double shift to save up some money for a real vacation for the two of them. Sam got her phone out and dialed her sister's work number. She was never allowed to pick up any calls while on the clock but she kept it on vibrate for emergencies. The phone rang three times before going to voicemail.

"Hey Missy, it's me, Sam. Call me as soon as you can. There's...weird stuff going on out there. Please, please call me immediately. You need to leave work right now and just go straight home and lock the doors."

A gunshot from inside.

"Shit! Winger, stay here and guard the truck." Sam jumped out and sprinted towards the house. She ran into the house and found Randall standing over a body.

"I had to shoot him. He was gonna kill me."

"Did he turn into one of them?" Sam already knew the answer to that. The smell finally hit her senses. She just wanted to confirm that he was in fact a zombie.

"Yeah, he did."

"You ok?" Sam stood next to Randall and put her hand on his shoulder.

"Yeah. Golden." He strapped the gun back into the holster and headed back towards the living room.

"What do we do now?" Sam asked as she followed him.

"I need to check the news." Randall clicked through the channels. Most of the networks were scrambled. Poor signal. When he finally picked up a channel, it only televised the same rehashed video that he saw at the gas station earlier that evening.

Sam had already gone online to check for alternative news. Word always spread faster on the internet and these days it seemed a more reliable and timely source.

"Randall, check this out."

He sat next to her as she turned the volume up. CNH - the Central News Hub had posted an article about the transformations that featured a user-submitted video of a young woman who recorded her own mother's transformation on film. The video concluded with her putting a bullet through the Sleeper, as she referred to it, right before she revealed that the Sleeper was in fact her own mother, bitten less than 8 hours ago.

Both Sam and Randall were speechless as they viewed the footage.

"This has gotta be a hoax." Randall shook his head.

"She's got a site." Sam clicked the link at the bottom of the post which redirected her to the video girl's site.

"Listen, we need to leave. Winger's probably freaking out in the truck and I really don't want to be here when the cops come. I'm sure the neighbors heard the gunshot and called the authorities by now."

"Fine. I'm taking this with me." Sam picked up the laptop and charger then walked towards the truck.

Randall looked around and didn't see any of the neighbor's lights on. "Maybe they didn't notice," he said.

"The cops aren't coming because they're too busy trying to manage a zombie apocalypse. God. That even sounds ridiculous coming from my mouth."

Sam hopped in the passenger seat, locked the door and flipped the laptop back open. Randall lit up a smoke as Sam played the next video. Randall listened in.

"Does she have a contact page with a number or something?" Randall asked.

"Lemme check." Sam clicked on a tab. "No number, just an email address."

"Write her a short note, tell her we want to meet. Put my name on it and leave my number."

Sam's fingers punched the keyboard as she wrote a quick note. "You think this girl's legit?"

"What's there to lose at this point? I don't even know where I'd go. She at least sounds like she's got some kind of a plan. I figured there's a 50% chance that she's telling the truth and she can help us deal with this shit..."

"Or?"

"Or, a 50% chance that she's a paranoid conspiracy theorist with absolutely no clue what to do. In which case, we just get the hell out of dodge and drive as far away from this mess as we can."

"It's probably like this everywhere."

"I'd like to think there's a safe haven out there, somewhere."

"Not to be a constant thundercloud but what if there isn't one?"

Randall knew there was a possibility of it being a hopeless run from their inevitable doom. We all die eventually. Matter of fact, right now, we're slowly dying. It's just a matter of what you do in between now and then. Randall has had an unhappy existence for as long as he could remember. He'd always been a cynic but lately he was more hopeful about the future. Maybe it was because of Sam being there. Maybe it was knowing that he'd have his own life and not be tethered to a toxic relationship with his father. He was unsure of what he would do with his new found freedom but he knew that he didn't want it to end like this. Somehow, he knew it would get better. There was something about Sam's question that wanted him to fight for survival. He placed his hand on Sam's. "Then we try our best to live as long as we can."

**

The snap of the latex gloves against her skin felt good as she slipped the other one on. She was just glad to feel anything at that point. It meant she was still alive.

She pulled the body off the bed by the ankles as the top end hit the wood floor with a thud. She rolled the body on to a plastic sheet, a clear shower liner from the second bathroom upstairs. She'd gotten the idea from the movie Psycho. Already tested and approved so why not? She rolled the body from the right edge of the liner to the left then secured both ends with twine to keep it from sliding out. The end product looked like a giant candy wrapper.

Now, for the hard part.

Collette lifted the bottom end and dragged it across the floor, outside of the bedroom, into the hallway, and down the stairs with the head thumping on each step. At the bottom of the staircase banister, a rifle hung by its shoulder strap. She slung it over and around her chest and continued with moving the corpse. She dragged it all the way outside and towards the fire pit between the house and the shed. Dragging a dead body on an unpaved dirt path was a lot harder than moving it on wood floor but at least it was well lit outdoors. Between the solar lights that lined the walkway and the motion lights planted along the side of the house, there was no need to turn anything else on.

It was a little past one in the morning and this probably could have waited until daylight but Collette wanted to get it done and over with. She wasn't worried about Sleepers spotting her mucking about in her yard with a giant bonfire. She was on the outskirts of town with a very low population count. On top of that, the electric fence was just installed not even a month ago and it's currently activated. The rifle around her chest was there just in case. You could never be too prepared. A cold breeze whipped the blaze around and intensified its fire. Collette knelt down in front of the plastic covered Sleeper.

"You deserved better than this." She rolled, lifted and heaved the body into the fire, took her gloves off and threw it into the blaze.

A red bandanna hung from around her neck. She pulled it up and over her mouth and nose then tightened the knot on the back. You only need to smell the burning decomposed body of a Sleeper once to know that you never want to catch a whiff of that again. This was her third burn. The first was the boy that bit her mother. The second was a random straggler who stood outside of the gate before she activated the fence. She didn't want it to get the attention of other Sleepers so she had to do something.

The heat from the pit felt good as it fed on its latest offering. It was another cold October night in Livingston County, Texas where the cold autumn air only made a brief appearance but when it did pay you a visit, you felt the chill all the way down to your bones.

She stepped away from the fire pit and watched the flames shoot up and out with fiery tendrils that reached out for her, luring her to inch in just a little closer.

That's it. Into the fire, little girl, where it's nice and warm.

Her eyes followed the puff of smoke that rose from the blaze and floated into the air then finally thinning out as it blended into the night sky.

Goodbye mom.

She followed the dirt trail back towards the house. There were a lot of things that needed to be done. Sometime between now and daylight she had to get some rest. But first, the cleanup continued.

Upstairs she wiped the blood and bits off the wall and off the headboard. She threw the rag into the middle of the bed then took the sheet off, wrapped it into a ball and threw it in a black trash bag. She wiped the floor with a pillowcase and threw that into the mix. She hauled the load outside and threw it in the pit.

There was no reason to live in filth even in a time of great uncertainty. Doing normal things during difficult times kept her calm and sane.

We're all just one bite away from being a Sleeper so it's best to be as civilized as possible while you still can, she recently wrote in a blog post.

After the cleanup she downed a bottle of water and checked on her messages online.

**

Since the first reports of the Sleeper attacks showed up on various media outlets, Collette had been campaigning to recruit, prepare and defend her town against the growing threat of this mystery virus. So far the only emails and phone calls she's received were from everyone else but her target audience. She'd been proposed to, been hired to report for an online zombie magazine, been condemned to hell, been asked for an interview, been invited to a premiere. The cherry on top of this bizarre flesh-eating cake was a phone call from a producer who offered her a role in a reality show.

Not one potential candidate to start a local militia. Zero.

**

First, she checked her emails. Inbox 55. She scanned through the subject and one jumped out of the page in particular.

Subject: Zombies are real. Just shot two tonight.

She clicked it open.

Watched your videos about Sleepers. Need your help. Not sure what else to do. We should meet. Randall 257-3574

She dialed the number and waited while she scanned more mail.

"Hello."

"Is this Randall?"

"Are you Parker Girl 85?"

"Yeah. It's Parkour Girl 85."

"What?"

"Never mind, I'll explain later. So you shot two Sleepers?"

"The zombies? Yeah, two of them. One was my dad."

"Sorry about that."

"Don't be. He was an asshole even before he tried to eat me."

"How do I know you're telling the truth?"

"I knew you were gonna say that so I just sent you a pic. Check your mail."

Inbox (New 1)

She clicked it open.

A photo of a dead Sleeper with a large part of its head missing, lying face down in a hallway.

"Did you get it?"

"Yeah. How long ago was this? Is this your house?"

"About 10 minutes ago. Yeah, it was my house."

"Who's we? And please tell me you disposed of the body. Don't just leave it there to rot."

"It's still there. It already smelled like it was rotten. Look, I don't wanna touch them if I don't have to. It doesn't matter anyway."

"First off, it's better to burn the bodies to prevent them from coming back. If it happened once, it may happen again. Second, who's we?"

"My girlfriend Sam and my dog Winger. We have an RV and we're probably just gonna bolt. Somewhere safe."

"Not sure if there is such a place anymore. If there is, it won't be that for long. Your best bet is to burn the body then meet me at my place. One more thing. This is important. Any of you got bitten or scratched open?"

"No."

"Good. Because if you are, I can't help you. I'll text you my address."

"We'll see you in a few," Randall said.

"Wait, if you have any weapons you can bring, anything at all, bring it with you."

"Got it. See ya."

**

"Well? What did she say?"

"She said burn the body then go to her place and take weapons with us if we have it."

"Burn the body," Sam repeated what he said, "that makes sense."

"Just in case they come back...you know."

"Are we coming back here afterwards?"

"Maybe. Not sure. Depends on what Prkrgrl85 says."

"Did you get her name?"

"No, I forgot to ask."

Altogether they returned to the house.

"Help me with this will ya?" Randall threw a blanket on Sleeper Doyle and wrapped him up with it. He grabbed one end with Sam on the other and took the body outside. Winger walked off to the side and kept quiet for once. He lifted the garage door open and fetched something inside while Sam waited. He returned with a large tin of lighter fluid. He popped the cap open and drizzled the contents all over the corpse. From his chest pocket he pulled out a box of matches.

"Do you want me to do this?" Sam asked.

"No, I got it. Step back a bit." He tugged on her sleeve and pulled her a few paces back with him.

He struck the match and threw it. Flames engulfed the blanket and the body inside. Randall couldn't contain himself as the smell of the burning corpse filled his senses. He buckled over to the side and vomited. Sam nearly did the same but was able to hold back.

Randall wiped his mouth with his sleeve and noticed the next-door neighbors had turned their lights on. From inside he could hear a sort of a scuffle, followed by breaking glass, followed by a man's scream. Then there was silence.

"We need to go. Let's grab a few things inside."

They grabbed as much as they can of Doyle's gun collection stashed away in his room. Sam stuffed the laptop in her backpack. Randall shut and locked the door behind them then ran towards the truck. Winger jumped into the back first, Sam hopped in the passenger seat. Randall, once again the pilot. The neighbor's front door opened and out came Mrs. Parnell with her blood-drenched yellow nightgown and a sleeping cap still on. Her mouth dripped of fluids from her last kill.

Randall started the engine as Mrs. Parnell tilted her head sideways then bolted towards the truck with a speed that shocked both Sam and Randall.

"Oh shit! She's headed this way. Go, go, go!" Sam yelled at Randall.

Randall stepped on the gas as Sleeper Parnell sprinted for the side of the truck closing in the gap. The truck had too much weight behind her with the RV hitched onto it and couldn't accelerate as fast.

"I'm gonna have to take a shot," Sam said.

"What? No! I can get rid of her. If you miss, she'll get to you."

"I won't miss. I can make the shot. Just trust me," Sam said as she rolled the window down, aimed for Sleeper Parnell's head and took the shot.

Sleeper Parnell's head jerked back as pieces of it flew off. It was like someone had pulled an invisible rug from underneath her. She fell on her back and stayed there as the truck gained speed. Sam rolled her window back up and stuck the gun in the holster.

"Shit, that was close. Nice shot though." Randall smiled at her.

"Thanks. My hand was shaking."

"Yeah, well, you still got her. That's all that counts. Doesn't have to be pretty."

"I just need some practice."

"Unfortunately, I think you'll be getting plenty of chances to practice."

"How long until we get there?"

"About 20-25 minutes. Depends on what's out there."

Sam leaned her head back on the headrest and closed her eyes. The tension on her shoulders loosened just a little. She didn't realize how tired she was until now. Her eyelids felt heavy and her head started to ache. Like the blood just rushed out of her head. It all finally sank in. The events of the past day, the transformed, the vicious attacks, the news reports, the deaths, and the uncertainty. It all hit her in a wave of pent up emotions and she found herself weeping.

Chapter 11: Versus

Helena came to on her own with her head propped up on a nice soft pillow and bundled up under layers of blanket. "Ugh, my head." She rubbed her temples and slowly pushed herself upright.

"Good, you're up." Cormac walked in and sat on the coffee table. "Made you some tea."

Helena took the cup from him and had a small sip. "This is good, thanks. How long have I been out?"

"Several hours. The sun should be out shortly. I was actually going to wake you up anyway."

"Why? Did you get some rest?" Helena set the cup down, leaned back on the couch and pulled the covers up to her neck.

"Yeah, just a little." He lied.

"Where are the kids?" She asked.

"Where we left them. Locked up in their room," he answered.

"Locked up?"

Oh god, she's forgotten all about it. Or she's in denial.

"Honey, don't you remember what happened to the twins? What Allen did to Dr. Meyers? Do you remember any of it?" He leaned forward and placed his hand on her knee.

She gazed at him for a few seconds and her facial expression changed from one that searched for an answer to one of recognition. She pursed her lips as her eyes welled up with tears.

Cormac squeezed her leg. "You remember now?"

She nodded her head in acquiesce. "My babies." She buckled into herself and sobbed as Cormac leaned forward and embraced her.

He held her in his arms for a few good minutes until the sobbing ceased and turned into sniffling. Cormac reached into his shirt pocket to retrieve a pill vial and pulled out an Ibuprofen from it. "Here take this for your headache."

Helena took it immediately. "So, what do we do now?" She asked.

"I need to go out and get a few things." He kissed her on the forehead and walked over to his favorite chair. He grabbed a black vest that hung on the backrest, slipped it on over his flannel shirt and zipped it up.

"You can't go out there Mac. Please don't leave us alone. We need you. I need you."

She still called him Mac. He hated it.

"I've been watching the news. I need to protect our home until we figure out where we can take the kids...to be cured, that is. We need more supplies, food, weapons. I think we're gonna be holed up here for a while and wait for this entire thing to blow over."

"We have a pantry full of food, Mac. That should be enough..."

"For a week, maybe two. We're going to need more than that babe."

"Please don't take too long."

"I won't. I don't know about you, but I'm starving. If you feel up to it you can fix something up while I do my run." He stroked her hair and smiled.

She returned the smile with a forced one. "Sure, I can do that."

"Whatever happens, do not let the children out of that room."

She looked up at him and nodded. "Ok."

"You promise me you'll keep it locked. Don't even go near that room. Do you understand? Promise me."

"I promise."

"Good. I've got my phone on me so keep yours by your side at all times. Keep this door locked and don't let anyone in. I'll be back shortly." He put his coat on and pulled his knit hat over his head. He unbolted, unchained and unlatched the locks and stepped outside.

The cold air snuck in and gave Helena the shivers even with a blanket draped around her shoulders. He already had the truck backed up. He rolled the window down and motioned for her to go back in and lock up. She shut the doors and latched, chained, and bolted the locks back on and walked over to the window. The dust kicked back behind his tires as he swung around and drove towards the front of the property.

Helena watched the truck disappear from view. In less than an hour the sun would be up. From the children's bedroom she heard scratching on the door.

You promised Cormac you wouldn't.

She walked back towards the couch when she heard them call.

"Mommy. Where are you?" It was little Alice who said it first. Then Allen said it too shortly after.

You promised.

"Mommy, we're hungry. Please let us out."

Helena's head ached again. The pressure from the back of her eyes increased.

Inside the children's bedroom, Alice and Allen scratched their nails across the wooden door. They enjoyed their last meal even if it were only a taste of what was to come. They stood there and moaned and grumbled. They sensed someone nearby. Muted footsteps turned into clear ones as the sound approached them. The Sleeper twins smelled their mother's scent from right outside the door. They salivated as the blisters around their mouths increased in size, some of them bursting open. The amount had multiplied threefold since the last feeding. They felt a dull pain almost simultaneously from the inside. They needed to feed again. Soon.

They groaned a little louder in unison.

**

Cormac decided to drive further into town to go to the new Mighty Warehouse. *The fewer stops I have to make, the better.*

The trip to the store was uneventful as he hoped it would be. The fact that they lived on the outskirts of town where everything was more spread out helped.

He prepared himself for the onslaught of traffic within the city limits. From about two traffic lights away he heard the sirens. The closer he drove towards it the more scattered it sounded. It came from all around him. There were abandoned cars by the side of the road. Some stalled vehicles up ahead slowed things down from where he was. He could see the lights of the store from the intersection. The streets had more vehicles than he expected but they all seemed to head for the highway. That's exactly what he would probably be doing by now had the children not been ill. Getting out of town. But this was Plan B. Stock up and stay put.

He turned into the parking lot only to swerve away from a van that nearly side swiped him as it sped out the wrong side of the road. One thing he did notice was the increase in foot traffic. There were people walking and running, some of them hobbled. People pushed their carts haphazardly in the middle of traffic. He heard the occasional screams. Cormac nearly turned his car around and headed back home but he knew he needed to get supplies. He put the car in park and popped the trunk. He fished out a wooden baseball bat from behind a duffel bag.

Just in case.

He had a game plan. Run in, get a few basic things and get out. He grabbed a cart on the way and pushed it through the sliding doors. Inside was a picture of total chaos. It was like the day before a major holiday and all the shoppers were scurrying to get last minute items or forgotten things. There were people from all directions moving in a dizzying pace. Only a couple of cashiers stood at their posts and they both had puzzled expressions on their faces.

"This is way outta hand, I'm about to leave this joint if the guards can't get this handled." One of them said to the other.

"Yeah, me too, I don't see what the big deal is, it's just another stupid flu virus." She shook her head, leaned on the counter and flipped through a magazine. They obviously haven't heard the reports.

Cormac pushed through the aisles and got what he needed. On the way back to the front of the store he heard a high pitched scream. He rushed towards it and saw the guard slumped on a bench holding his wrist which bled profusely. His face was scrunched up in a twisted agony as a couple of employees tended to him.

"That guy just bit Bernie!" One cashier pointed out a man that already hobbled his way outdoors.

The cashiers spotted the store manager and followed him to the office. There were at least six people standing in line in both stations.

"Hey, can somebody check us out over here?" One guy said.

Two ladies started chatting with each other. "Can you believe this service? I'm never shopping here again." A lady with poofy hair said.

"I'm gonna be calling their headquarters and putting in a complaint. Heads will roll." Another lady who had a very strong cheap perfume on said.

A couple of people with only a few things in a basket decided that the lack of staff manning their station meant that they were entitled to the goods free of charge.

"They're not here to check me out, then I'm walking out with my groceries. Fuck this." One man justified his theft and walked right out. Two more people followed suit when they noticed that no one stopped the previous looters.

"If they're gonna do that and get away with it then I can too." The old man said.

Cormac was next in line. He looked around and scanned the area for any red-shirt employee but saw none. He dug through his wallet and pulled out a wad of bills, reached over the counter and threw it in a shelf. "Here, there's plenty enough money there to cover what I have." He rolled his cart out towards the car, popped his trunk and loaded everything up as fast as he can. Behind him he heard a low groan. He grabbed the baseball bat out of the cart and turned around. A Sleeper stood in front of him. A female teenager with her messenger bag still slung across her chest. Stringy blond, blood-stained hair obscured her face. Fresh blood dripped from her chin and down towards her argyle sweater. Cormac pushed the empty shopping cart and used it to pin her on the back of someone else's van. He gripped the base of the bat tightly and drew his arms back over his head. He aimed for the girl's head and was about to strike when a gunshot rang from his left side. The Sleeper girl's head jerked as the bullet entered one side of her head and exited the other. Brain matter and blood splattered the van and the sidewalk.

"It's easier with a gun." A female walked over to the fallen body and fired another shot at the head. "I like to be sure," she said to Cormac.

"Thanks."

"No problem. Firearms work best. An arrow to the head works fine too. Actually, any trauma to the head is effective. Take care of yourself." The woman sprinted across the lot and into her vehicle. Just like that, she was gone.

Cormac, still stunned by what just happened got into his car and headed back home.

**

She'd been sitting on the floor with her back against the door for about half an hour now. They asked her to tell them a story and she did. Word for word she recited a couple of their favorites to help them pass the time. Her head buzzed with an intense ache the whole time. Closing her eyes helped but not by much. She was unaware that they've connected with her mentally, since she first woke up from her sleep. They've slowly strengthened the bond through manipulation of memories. The more she was willing to reciprocate, the easier it was for them to grab a hold of her and drag her into the rabbit hole.

"Mommy, why did daddy leave us here?" Alice asked Helena. Only it was actually a groan.

"Because he's trying to find a cure. He wants both of you to feel better. That's why," she answered.

"That's what he told you mommy. He lied. He locked us in here because he hates us. He said we're the reason he's not a successful writer. His life would be different, would be better if we were never born," Allen told his mother.

"No, that's not true. He would never say that. He loves you both. Now you should sleep and get some rest." Helena's chest tightened. She knew there was a seed of truth in what they said. Some things didn't have to be said out loud. She felt it from him.

"Mommy, we're really tired. Can you tuck us in? Please."

"I can't. I promised your daddy I wouldn't."

The children wept and sobbed. Helena could bare it no longer. Her children needed her. She wept along with them.

Where are you Mac?

"Please mommy. We don't feel good. Please tuck us in. And tell us another story."

Helena unlooped the chain from the doorknob and the chair. She moved the chair aside and opened the door slightly. Alice and Allen reached their hands out to their mother. Helena stepped into their room and held their hands. Allen closed the door behind her.

"Tell us a story mommy. We're so very hungry."

They led her towards the bed where she sat, flanked by the children.

"Once upon a time..."

They salivated and sank their teeth into her arms.

**

Cormac pulled up next to the house and unloaded the trunk. He hung the plastic bag handles through the baseball bat which worked well in saving him time from having to make multiple trips to the car. He carried it and set it down on the porch as he rang the bell. "Helena, baby, it's me. I'm home. I need some help with the groceries."

There was no answer. He rang the bell again a little longer this time and followed it up with a couple of strong knocks on the door. Still no answer. He heard nothing from inside.

Maybe she fell asleep.

He got his keys out and unlocked the first two bolts. He pushed the door open which was abruptly stopped by the third lock - the chain.

"Shit."

He pounded on the door with his fist.

"Helena, wake up. Unhook the chain please." He hollered through the crack. Helena was a light sleeper. If a mosquito entered the room she'd wake up. There was no way she didn't hear that last knock.

Something's wrong he thought although he tried to adapt the Think Positive mantra, something inside, deep from his guts, told him otherwise.

He shouldered the door a few times but the chain held in place. He stepped back a few paces and charged towards the door, making contact with it with speed and all of his weight behind it this time. The chain broke off its hinge, the door flew wide open and slammed into the wall, and Cormac stumbled into the living room. He was able to brace himself from falling with the back of a chair. Helena wasn't on the couch. The teacup sat on the table half-empty. It was too quiet. So quiet that he could hear the humming of the fridge from the next room over. He went back out on the porch to retrieve the bat as he headed towards the children's bedroom.

"Helena! Where are you baby?"

The chair was still chained to the doorknob where he had left it. He would've been relieved to see that if it hadn't been for the blood smeared on the door knob, the chain, the chair, and the door itself. The children heard his voice and banged on the door. He flinched and gripped the base of the bat with both hands. There was a trail of blood drips that led him down the hallway and towards their master bedroom. In the bedroom, the blood drips continued into the master bath. He could see the light was on and he heard some noise coming from that direction.

"Helena, is that you?"

He stood in front of the bathroom door which was half-open. He pushed it open with the tip of the bat and saw Helena. She stood in front of the vanity wrapping a long piece of gauze around her right forearm in the same manner as she had wrapped her left forearm. The blood had already partially seeped through the bandage on the left one.

Cormac was frozen in place.

Without looking at him she continued to twist and turn the long piece of bandage around her arm.

"What took you so long, dear? The children were hungry. So I gave them what they wanted." She told him in a monotonous voice.

"Helena, what have you done?" Cormac asked.

"You left us on our own. I fed my babies."

"They're sick. And you let them bite you. That means you have it now. You were supposed to wait for me."

She turned towards him as she held both arms out. She tilted her head in an unnatural, awkward manner. Her face had already changed. She had a gaunt appearance to her now. Even her skin didn't seem right. Not pale, but gray. A desaturated shade. Small blisters had already formed around her mouth.

"I'm so very tired Mac. I think I'm gonna lie down and sleep for a while. Why don't you join me?"

Cormac shook his head. "I'm sorry I have to do this." He shut the bathroom door, grabbed the chair from the corner and hooked it under the doorknob. He sprinted towards the kitchen junk drawer and pulled out another bike chain, the one for Helena's mountain bike. He hurried back into the room and looped it around the door knob and the back of the chair.

"Let me out of here Mac! I just need some sleep." She banged on the door.

"I can't," he answered back.

He stepped out of the room and shut the door behind him. With bat still in hand he walked past the children's room, past their growling little faces. He could have sworn he heard their voices as he passed by.

"You really didn't think we'd let you have her, do you?" The children's voices mocked him.

He heard them giggle. He felt a sharp pain in his head right then. He shook it off and headed towards the front of the house. The groceries sat where he last left them. He felt so tired and wanted to just lie down and sleep but he was too afraid he'd never wake up. Or worse, he'd wake up and be like them. He looked out at his property which stretched a couple of acres out, the tree-lined border up ahead hid the main road on the other side. The sun just now broke through the night sky, bands of light magenta scattered across the clouds. Over to the left the fog crawled its way closer to the house. An eerie scene to start the new day. Cormac leaned on the door frame with furrowed brows and a heavy heart. He felt so tired. How long can one go on with an empty tank? His wife and kids turned into cannibalistic monsters and he had no idea what to do about it.

Maybe I should just join them.

The morning sun felt good on his skin. He shook the self-defeating thoughts out of his head and reached down into one of the bags and pulled out an energy drink. He dialed a number on his phone. The main number to get in touch with Toller has been rerouted back to Mission Control. He thought that was strange.

A beeping from his laptop. He'd forgotten to sign off from earlier. He walked over and flipped it open. A new message in his inbox from Prkrgrl85. He clicked it open.

Hello future freedom fighter,

Thank you for your email. We should meet. Call me at my number below for details.

~Prkrgrl85

Chapter 12: Instructions

The country road was paved with rough gravelly patches. It stretched out ahead of her flanked by ranch land. She'd passed by the same houses and buildings that have been there forever. With the exception of maybe a new drive-through bank next to the well-lit gas station slash general store, everything pretty much stayed the same. She hadn't been back in this area of town since she left. It felt like she was driving through a ghost town.

Alli drove down that road for about a mile then slowed to a stop next to a mailbox that appeared to have been recently painted in primary green with the address stenciled in white. She turned right and drove up to the gate and was surprised to see someone already there to meet her. The electric gate slid open as the man stepped aside and waved her in. A great dane and a basset hound quietly stood by him.

She rolled the window halfway down. "Hi dad."

"Hi there baby girl. I've been expecting you."

"You have?"

"Yep. Just park your car over there, pick a spot. I'll be right behind ya." He hopped on to his golf cart as Alli parked under the carport.

She got out of the car and gave him a big hug.

"You look different," she said. He was thinner than she remembered. No, not thin. Leaner. She was used to seeing him with a beard which was now all gone. His hair had more silver streaks than it used to. It was also longer and slicked back. If he had not been standing there with a cane and his nearly threadbare work vest she would have taken him for a stranger.

"Good to have you back home." He told her in his usual gruff voice as he patted her back. They went in through the side door and the smell of freshly brewed coffee permeated the air. She settled down at the breakfast nook. She ran her fingers across the naturally distressed table top. It still had a carving of her name on it with a smiley face drawn underneath.

"You carved that when you were nine years old." He poured himself a cup and was about to pour one for her.

"None for me dad, thanks. I'll have some juice if you have any."

Her dad crinkled his forehead and squinted his eyes.

"Don't look at me like that. I'm just trying to eat healthy."

"Since when?" He smirked.

"Since I found out I'm gonna be eating for two."

A big shit-eating grin spread across his face. "You mean I'm gonna be a grampaw?"

She nodded and smiled. He poured her a glass of orange juice with pulp.

"That's just somethin' else. I mean, it's wonderful." He kissed her on top of her head and sat down across from her.

She took a sip of her juice. "So how did you know I was coming?"

"I taught you well enough to know in times of trouble to find the most secure place you can think of. And based on what I've seen on the news and online, I'd consider this as one of those times." He spooned a couple of heaps of sugar into his cup, poured some milk and stirred it.

"I've seen those things up close. Ben got bit and..."

"He turned into a monster." Her dad cut her off. "Did he scratch or bite you anywhere?"

"No. I shot him and ran to my car. Didn't seem to affect him any, he ran after me."

"You gotta aim for the head next time." He slurped on his coffee and set it down. "For some reason their weak spot is their head or brain or whatever."

"How do you know all this?"

"Been digging up some info. I've read some things. Seen some things. Not really surprised this is going down." He stroked his chin like he was scratching a phantom beard.

"Come on, dad. Don't start with your theories."

"Hey, you asked."

"I guess I did."

"You should get some rest, you look exhausted."

"So do you."

"You sleep first. I need to keep guard. Then maybe we'll switch."

"Dad, thanks for just...being here."

"That's what daddies are for."

"With everything that's happened, I thought you'd be upset."

"That's in the past now."

"Still. I'm sorry."

"You know I did try to get a hold of you once but your number changed."

"Yeah, I got a new phone. I wasn't sure if you even wanted to talk to me."

"I always want to talk to you. I just don't like that asshole you ran off with."

"Well, I don't think you'll have to worry about him anymore."

"Actually, yeah I do. He's still walking around somewhere."

"In his condition someone will either run him off or shoot him before he gets anywhere. I doubt he'd know where to go."

But he does. They're smarter than they look. He didn't want to alarm his daughter any more than she already was.

They sat there in silence drinking their beverages, lost in their own thoughts. The kitchen clock's ticking suddenly seemed loud.

"What's going on out there? People just don't all of a sudden wake up and decide they want to eat other people," she asked. Up till that moment she didn't have a chance to reflect on everything that's happened for the last 24 hours. There wasn't any time to process it all. Now she struggled to make sense of the irrational.

He wanted to explain the answer in a way that was straightforward, fact-based and brief. He had collected enough information to run a seminar on it but that wouldn't do. "Remember that odd storm that hung around these parts for some time? That's how it started."

She looked at him with confused eyes. He could almost see the wheels turning in her head.

"Wait. Let me finish before you say something. Just bear with me." He leaned forward placing his elbows on the table, closing in the gap between the two of them as if he was about to reveal a secret.

"Anyone who was exposed to that rain long enough was instantly infected. The disease isn't airborne but if enough made contact with your mucous membrane then it was able to penetrate in that manner. Now, I don't know how much rain it took to get someone sick but probably not much. Shortly after that, people would sleep and stay asleep. This is when they transform. They wake up from this sort of coma and all of a sudden their entire biological makeup had changed and devolved into something primal. They craved raw meat to satiate their hunger and relieve their pain. The way they reproduce is through spreading the disease. They develop blisters all over their body but predominantly around their mouth and fingertips. The blisters secrete the fluid which serves as a transport between hosts. If they bite you or scratch you and it breaks skin, then you've been infected."

"You realize how this sounds right?"

"Yeah, but it's true. It's not common knowledge yet but the information is floating around out there."

"And you just happen to come across it."

He shook his head in frustration. "There are some things you don't know about me."

"Like what?"

He sighed. "Look, I think it's better if we talked about this later."

"You expect me to sleep after what you just told me? Besides, there may not be a later."

"Let's just say that I...me...along with a small group of people were contracted to work on a highly classified project a long time ago."

"Oh."

"You sound disappointed."

"I thought you were gonna tell me you're an alien from another planet, the mother ship is back and they're here to destroy all humans." She chuckled and expected him to do the same. Instead, he looked at her with a serious expression on his face.

"Dad, it was a joke."

"It's not funny because you're partly right."

"You're kind of freaking me out right now."

"Good! Because this is some serious stuff I'm telling you and you should be paying close attention to what I'm saying." He addressed her with a raised voice and the same tone he used back when she lived here and slacked on her chores.

"I'm sorry. I'm sorry."

"As I was saying..."

"So, you're a spy?!"

"No. Nothing of the sort. I did research work regarding lost civilizations."

"So this whole 'I'm a handyman' was just a guise?"

"No. The other part just happened to be my job before you were born. I left when I found out your mom was pregnant."

"So what's this classified project you worked on?"

"I was getting to that. While we worked at the university we were commissioned by the

Department of Defense to take part in an intensive study that involved us staying within containment for six months. We weren't given the details prior, only that we would be generously compensated for our contribution. We were young, eager, and curious, not to mention underpaid so we jumped at the offer. Your mother and I had only been dating for a couple of months. She wasn't too thrilled about me being away for that long but she realized how critical it would be for my career. All I remember was that we all had to take a pill and the next time I opened my eyes, I was alone in a small room with a binder next to me containing instructions to what we had to do while we were in there. "

"So you were locked in that room for six months?"

"No, that became our living quarters. All three of us got one. What was outside our bunkers changed all our lives that day."

"Dad, what was it?"

"It was a fully reconstructed annex of an ancient library. They didn't tell us anything about it, or how they managed to transport monolithic sized stones inside that facility. We weren't allowed to ask questions. Our primary task was to decipher and translate the text for one selected book. We were provided notes and findings from previous teams who have done their part. "

"You said the Department of Defense commissioned you guys."

"Correct."

"What do they have anything to do with ancient relics and translating old books?"

"I'm glad you're asking the right questions." He cracked a sly grin.

"So did your crew figure it out?"

"Yes, we were successful in finishing the translation. And I know what you're gonna ask me. What was so important about that one book? I know, because that's the very question we all asked from day one. It was a book of instructions."

"Instructions for what?"

"How to destroy all humans."

She started to ask another question but he cut her off. "The rest of that story will have to wait. You need to get rest while you can."

"Fine. Just one more thing. What exactly is the plan now?"

"The plan is to hunker down here. It's safe. I've got plenty of firearms and ammunition. Stocked up on supplies. Enough for five years for two people and two hungry doggies. Got a live fence wrapped all around this property. Surveillance cameras hooked up. Motion lights. And of course, a bunker."

"Um, you've been busy."

"Had to keep myself occupied with both my girls gone."

"Wait, did you just say you have a bunker?"

"Yes. Yes, I did. We do have a bunker."

"When you say bunker, you don't mean the underground kind do you?"

He nodded his head. "Uh-huh. That's exactly what I'm talking about."

"Since when?"

"It was there when I got the house. I just made slight alterations throughout the years."

"Did mom know?"

He nodded.

"How can I not have known about this?"

"Because your daddy is one sneaky monkey."

"Be serious dad."

"I'm being serious. I worked on it every day."

"So where is it exactly? How do you get to it?"

Her dad pointed down to the ground. "We're sitting right above it. The entrance is over at the back. I'll give you a grand tour after you get some rest."

"I've got so many questions about this and about what's going on out there. My head's hurting."

"First, sleep. Then we talk."

"Ok."

"I got your bed ready for you."

"Thanks dad." She got up and hugged him. "Love you."

"Love you too. Sweet dreams."

She walked into her old room where nothing's been touched. She turned on her lamp and it projected constellations onto the ceiling directly above it. She ran her fingers past the books on the shelf leaving a trail where she had wiped the dust off. She grabbed a plush giraffe toy off a window bench and crawled into bed with it. She pulled the covers up to her neck and immediately felt herself drifting to sleep. Her mind was filled with images of the day, questions about the past and concerns for the future. Finally, she surrendered to exhaustion.

**

He peeked into Alli's room and was relieved to find her finally getting some rest. He had poured himself another cup of coffee and headed into his office to continue the work he was doing before his daughter arrived.

The Department of Defense may have kept the original documents from that day but he remembered every single word of it. They were unaware of his eidetic memory. He had committed the entire instruction codex as well as additional related materials to memory and was in the final stages of translating and transcribing it using the

English language. Soon, he'd be able to forward the document to his contact.

Chapter 13: Reboot

"You have arrived at your destination." The GPS announced as they pulled up in front of a gated entrance. There was a panel outside that for buzzing in. Surveillance cameras were planted above both sides of the gate. Randall saw the flashing red light as it swiveled around slowly. The truck moved forward slightly as Randall rolled the window down. He reached out and pressed the faded red button. Sam noticed the plume of smoke that rose from the property but said nothing about it to Randall.

"Identify yourself." A female voice blurted from the speaker.

"Randall Woods. I spoke with you about half an hour ago."

"The gate will open in a second, just follow the driveway, I'll meet you outside."

Randall drove down at a slow pace and followed the driveway as instructed. "I hope she's got coffee made, I'm about to pass out I'm so tired."

"I'd rather take a nap," Sam answered.

"Yeah. Definitely a nap. Then coffee."

The house they came to was a typical home for this region. An older house with white shingles all throughout and a wrap-around porch. Over to the side the fire pit continued a slow burn.

A woman with long dark hair stood on the top step of the porch. She wore a standard issue military fatigues and a black jacket. A firearm hung from her right shoulder.

"Here goes nothing," Randall said as he put the truck on park and killed the engine. "You guys ready?"

Sam had Winger in her arms and was already halfway out the truck.

"I guess so," Randall said to himself as he trailed Sam.

"I'm Sam. This is Winger. She's mostly harmless." They shook hands.

"I'm Collette. I'm mostly harmless too, unless there's Sleepers around."

Randall nodded and was going to say something when a slight breeze blew the fire pit smoke towards where they stood. One whiff was all it took for both Sam and Randall to identify what was burnt. Both coughed and shielded their noses. Winger whined and panted.

"Let me guess...you've been barbecuing zombies over there haven't you?"

"Yeah, just a few. Still can't get used to that smell so I wear this usually." She tugged on her bandanna that hung from around her neck. "Come in, we have a lot to cover."

**

Randall and Sam sat on the couch with Winger parked in between. Collette already had a nice blaze going in the fireplace. The warmth felt good and made it difficult for both to stay alert and awake. It also gave the appearance of normalcy. A warm and cozy farmhouse amidst a zombie outbreak. Collette walked in carrying a serving tray with a carton of fruit juice and some crackers. She set it down on the large wooden coffee table and sat on the couch across from them.

"Just a light snack for now. The pasta should be ready shortly. Please, help yourselves."

Collette looked younger in person. She had long dark hair, pale skin, dark eyes. She carried herself with a deep level of intensity and seriousness that made those around her feel slightly uneasy. Randall and Sam were no exception to this.

Sam had already drunk half the glass of juice.

"Juice and biscuits sound really quaint but I need something stronger. You got any coffee? Something to keep me awake," Randall asked.

Sam nudged him with her elbow and glared at him. "Sorry, he's always cranky," she said to Collette.

"Coffee will give you a temporary boost. You have to start thinking long-term," Collette said to Randall.

"Not sure how long we all have with those creeps outside eating everyone."

"As long as we can fight and exterminate them all then we'll be fine. Speaking of, did you guys come across any on your way here?"

"Not really," Sam answered. "There weren't mobs of them walking in groups if that's what you meant.

Randall chugged down the juice. "What do you mean about long-term?"

"As I've stated on my videos, I'm in the process of assembling a militia to regain control of this town. What you've seen so far is nothing compared to what's to come. The more people I can get together to fight this thing, the better our chances of survival is. According to my parents' report, if this continues to spread at this rate, North America will be overtaken by Sleepers in less than a month. We don't have much time so I need your undivided attention. I have to educate you about Sleepers and train you to defend and attack when accosted."

"Why don't we just leave it to the military to worry about it?"

"Because they're not coming."

"You don't know that for sure."

"No, I don't. But I don't like the fact that you're so willing to hand over your fate on the grounds that you think someone will rescue you."

"I don't like your tone and I don't appreciate what you're implying." Randall stood up. "Sam, let's go. We don't need anyone's help."

Sam remained seated. "I'm not going anywhere until I get some answers. This is why we came here for and we're gonna stay here until she's through talking. You can go if you want but I'm not moving."

Randall sat back down and motioned Collette to continue.

"The first generation Sleepers got the disease from that recent storm. Exposure to rain. Just like any illness, some people were more prone to catching it. Once they were infected, they went into a cocoon stage where all they do was sleep. Their bodies died, normal functions ceased but something else takes over. They wake up very hungry, confused and in pain. It only takes a short time to figure out that the pain goes away after they've consumed raw meat. From that initial high they seek out what they need at all costs. For some cases they establish a psychic link with the ones they were close to when they were living. Not always, but some. My father's theory was that the first and second generation Sleepers had this skill but then it becomes watered down as it gets passed on. Each Sleeper is as unique as its previous life. Who they were before - age, health, intelligence, determines how they will be when they've turned. Their primary drive is to consume. Secondary is to multiply. It's more of a plague really. If they succeed they'll turn the world's population into them and exhaust their food supply. They'll starve to death eventually leaving the earth practically uninhabited by humans."

"Extinction," Sam said.

"Pretty much." Collette poured herself some juice and took a couple of gulps. "Any questions?" She directed the question to Randall first then turned to Sam as well.

The couple looked at each other then back at Collette. The expression on their faces revealed what words could not.

"I'll just keep talking then." Collette got up and fed the fireplace a few more logs. "The worst thing a person can do at this time is to sit there and not do anything. It would be just a matter of time until they get to you. If we form a local militia and set an example for splinter groups to form then we just may have a fighting chance." She crouched by the fire and warmed her hands.

"How come you know all this?" Randall asked. "Sounds kind of suspicious to me."

"That's the first smart thing that came out of your mouth." She waited for him to take the bait.

Randall was about to give her a piece of his mind when Sam grabbed his arm. "Shut up Randall. Don't you see she's just trying to press your buttons?"

"You should listen to her Randy, she speaks the truth." Collette smirked.

Sam stood up and put her hand on her knife which snuggly rested on her belt sheathe. "As for you, one more wisecrack and you'll have a knife embedded right in the middle of your heart so fast you won't even realize you're already dead. I'm exhausted, I can't get a hold of my sister, and there are fucking zombies walking out there who wants to have me for a snack. I'm really not in the mood for smart-ass comments and mind games. So carry on with your story without it."

Sam's outburst took Collette by surprise. "Alright, fair enough. But just so you know, I haven't exactly had a peachy kind of last couple of days either. I watched my mother turn into a Sleeper and I had to shoot her then burn her. On top of that I've been trying to round up people to join me in this fight but no one seems to be fucking interested." She got up and walked up to Sam, invading her personal space. Randall sensed the volatile tension that was about to explode and get really ugly so he stepped in between the two to break it up.

"Whoa, whoa. Time out. Everyone needs to take a quick breather. We've all had it rough as of late so let's just turn it down a notch and try to work together. This is why we're all here now. We're fighting those people snackers not each other. Remember?"

The two women stared each other down for just a little while longer before backing up.

"So you got an answer for Randall's question?" Sam asked.

"My parents took part in a classified research back in the day. There were three of them altogether that took over. They were there for six months, all locked up. They translated this ancient document from a lost civilization, my father called it Instructions and it explained how to eliminate mankind. The people that hired them didn't think they'd be able to piece it all together within that time but they did and only told their employer part of it for fear that their lives would be endangered. Since then all three of them had made plans to prepare for the day that the government would figure out the rest of the text and put it to use. You guys with me?"

"Why would an entire civilization want to exterminate themselves? That doesn't make sense," Randall asked.

"I asked my folks the same thing. Their theory was that the elders in charge of this secret weapon deemed it right to reboot and start over."

"So now the government knows how to manipulate this?" Sam asked.

"I guess so. Think about it. If it worked once to eliminate an entire civilization then the possibilities for warfare for those who harness its powers is limitless."

"Yeah, but why wage war on your home turf?" Randall said as he put a half-smoked cigarette in his mouth. "Is it alright to smoke in here?"

"Yeah, that's fine," Collette said. "Maybe it was accidental."

"That makes sense. That's why there's no help coming our way. They'd have to answer to the general public. They'll implicate themselves," Sam said.

"One hell of an accident huh?" Randall took a long drag. "So where's your dad?"

"He passed away a few years ago. When he fell ill he talked to my mom about telling me everything they knew. So that's how I was able to prepare. I've spent all my money and my time for this cause since then."

"So what's the master plan, Chief?" Randall leaned on the mantle and threw the cigarette butt in the fireplace.

"A bit of training. Need to give you a tour of this place. Get more people to join us, for starters. But first, get some rest. You'll need it." Collette took a wrought iron poker and pushed around the burning logs, embers scattering in all directions. "Past the kitchen there's four rooms with cots in it. Take your pick." A muffled ringing came from Collette's cargo pocket. She walked off away from the couple as she picked up the call.

"This is surreal," Sam said to Randall as they started heading out towards the rooms.

"Straight out of a movie. Come, Winger." Randall patted the side of his leg twice. Winger hopped off the couch and pranced right behind him. They were halfway into the kitchen when Collette called out.

"Hey guys?" She spoke with a smile on her face as she slipped her phone back in her pocket. The first authentic expression she's had since they've arrived here. "Got another one on board. Some guy named Cormac. He said he's headed this way. Just thought I'd tell you."

"The more the merrier. Wake us up if you need back-up," Randall replied.

Collette headed upstairs to the study and settled in front of the laptop. A barrage of new emails awaited her attention but she was more interested in one in particular. She scanned the contents of her inbox and spotted what she was looking for. She clicked it open and downloaded the contents.

Chapter 14: Translations

She found her dad in his office. He'd fallen asleep on his chair. She walked over to his desk which was well-organized. Everything in its place. A stack of folders sat on one corner. An old coffee mug that said #1 Dad on it (a gift she gave him back in grade school) was filled with pens and pencils. She picked up a picture frame with a family photo taken when the fair was in town. She must have been seven years old in it. She had overalls on over a white and pink shirt. She sat on her dad's lap holding a half-eaten cotton candy stick. Her mom had her arm draped over her dad's shoulder.

"Had a good sleep?"

She flinched and set the picture down. "Yeah, actually I did. I needed that. You?"

"Shoot. At this age, it don't make much of a difference if I get 10, 20, 30 hours of sleep. I still feel old when I wake up." He stretched his arms sideways.

"Could be worse," Alli said.

"Yeah, you're right. I could wake up and start eating people. Puts things into perspective don't it?"

Alli grinned. "So. How about that tour of the bunker now?"

**

Outback they stood in front of the old wooden playhouse he built for her as a kid.

"What are we doing here?" She asked him.

"You said you wanted to see the bunker and I'm showing you." He pulled the little door open. "After you."

She looked at him, puzzled, but curious. She crouched down and walked in the playhouse. Her dad was right behind her.

"Here, put this on." He handed her a headlamp. His was already turned on. He shut the door behind him and started to move some floor planks around. Alli placed the headlamp on her head and switched it on.

"Stack these over on that side." He handed her each wood strip and she carefully placed it where he had asked her to.

"Damn. I thought I'd built this playhouse large enough." He muttered to himself.

"You did. We just got larger."

"I'll pretend I didn't hear you say that." He pulled the last plank out of the center and revealed a four foot by three foot area. He kicked aside a layer of dirt at a certain spot which revealed a latch. He placed both hands on it and pulled down. A muted thump noise was followed with what sounded like a hiss.

"I never get tired of that sound." He searched for something near the edge of where the planks slipped in. He brushed some dirt aside and pulled on two handles in opposite corners. "You can get down now but wait for me at the first landing. Watch your step."

She reached the bottom of the steps and waited for her dad to descend. A couple of small bluish LED lights illuminated the landing. It wasn't overly bright but illuminated enough of the surroundings to see what's around you. A large door that looked a lot like an entrance to a vault was right in front of her. He turned the wheel clockwise three times and pulled. It was a bulky, thick, heavy duty door with a giant deadbolt lock. Her dad signaled her to enter.

She peeked in and saw nothing but darkness. She couldn't make anything out from standing outside. "I don't know about this."

"It's safe, just walk in and the lights will switch on automatically. Go on."

She took a few steps forward and the motion lights, similar to the ones on the landing but slightly brighter, clicked on. The first thing she saw looked like a hotel lobby. A couple of club chairs to the right with a large colorful abstract painting above and behind it. To the left was a framed image. She walked over to it and realized it was a blueprint, a map, to the bunker. She heard the thump of the door shutting.

"This place has enough room for a dozen people according to this," she said to him as he stood next to her.

"Yeah, ample room to stay comfortable."

"You said this was already here when you bought the house. Why would anyone have a bunker this size here?"

"The question is why not? One can..."

"Never be too prepared," Alli interjected. That was one of her father's favorite mantra. "So all this is right underneath the house?"

"That's correct. About twenty five feet below." He started walking towards the entry way. "There's plenty more to see than that map."

She followed him through the maze of hallways. "I expected something different from this."

"Is that good or bad?"

"No, it's good. I thought it was gonna be like being inside a vault. You know...cold steel, industrial. This is homey."

"That's exactly what I was going for. I figured if we were gonna be stuck in here then we needed to feel like this was home. You should've seen it before. It was depressing. I tried to sleep here for one night just to test it out. I couldn't stand it."

"You did a great job dad." She patted him on the shoulder.

He led her into one of the sleeping chambers. The setup pretty much followed the same formula for each - a bunk bed, a small desk with shelves above it, a small reading lamp and a footlocker. Each room had a laptop. In between rooms were a couple of small bathrooms with a shower area. A galley kitchen to the right with a 1950s retro dining room set next to it. The walk-in pantry was fully stocked with provisions, an extra set of folding chairs and table was up against one wall. The hub of the bunker was set up like a large living area. Couches, a couple of cushy club chairs set up in almost semi-circle formation. A television and media cabinet in front of it. Another hallway up past that led you to a small library area with floor to ceiling shelves filled with books on every subject. A couple of chairs, floor lamps, small side tables and an area rug gave the room a finished look. Adjacent to the library was a small clinic with a couple of stretchers and a supply cabinet. Across from it was an area enclosed in glass. The lighting in there was different and brighter.

"This is to simulate actual sunlight. Still not the same as catching some rays outside but I felt it was a necessity to keep our minds healthy. Cabin fever and lack of sunlight can do things to your mental health. They had something similar to this over at that facility I was telling you about. Come in, have a seat."

They sat in an area with mismatched patio furniture. The chaise style chair Alli sat in was comfortable. They faced a wall lined with potted plants. Tucked in between was a large water feature - a wall of stones with cascading water.

Her dad pointed to it. "You know that fountain is actually hooked up to the generator. Back there is a door. I built a little dog run for Hera and Penny. Don't get too comfy. The tour's not over yet."

He led her towards the end of the hallway. It was another heavy duty door but not as impressive as the main entrance. This was old and had a weathered appearance. Her dad pulled out a set of keys from his jacket and unlocked it.

"This part of the tour may not be of interest to you. Kind of technical, where the inner workings of everything is. But it's something you need to know how to operate." He stepped in first and the lights turned on. It's a narrow rectangular room with panels on one side, generators lined up with a tangle of wires running from one side of the room to the other. Switches and knobs that controlled the surveillance camera. A couple of old fashioned radio and communications kit.

"It looks like a mess but this is actually pretty organized. It'll take me about an hour or two to go over everything here. The manuals for each are on that shelf over there. The originals are there but I also took the time to rewrite some things so that the average person can walk in here and be able to perform routine maintenance or even minor repairs if need be."

"I've got a lot of reading to do it seems," she answered.

"Funny you should say that." He unzipped his jacket partway down and pulled out a stack of papers and handed it over to his daughter. "Before anything else, you need to read these two things. And when you're through reading it, read it again.

Then read it again. Commit it to memory if you can."

She flipped through the stack which was divided into two books, held together by cheap report covers. The first one simply entitled *Instructions: Project Reboot.*

The second one: *How to start a revolution. The book of resistance.*

"Is this what I think it is?" She asked as she skimmed through the first few pages of the first report.

"It is. In your hands is the first ever print rendition of an ancient lost civilization's instructions on how to destroy the world, fully translated in English."

"You remembered everything?"

He pointed at his temple. "Eidetic memory."

"And this second book?"

"That was a different book that I secretly read while I was in the facility. It was a risky thing to do but we all decided it was just as important as what we were there to work on. This was about being a

freedom   fighter.   Hope   amidst   absolute
destruction."

"Good versus evil," she said to him. "So we're
one of the good guys then."

"You could say that." He stroked his imaginary
beard again. "It's not always that simple. I imagine
you have many questions. We should head up and
discuss things above ground."

**

They resurfaced and arranged the planks back
on top of the entryway. Outside the playhouse the
sun hid behind grey clouds.

"The whole time I played here when I was a
kid, never knowing what was right under my feet."

"I couldn't risk telling you, you'd go to school
and tell everyone about it."

"If the bunker was here after you bought the
house, who did it belong to?"

"An old war vet who continued what his father
built.   They   were   unable   to   maintain   this
homestead   at   their   age   so   they   needed   to

downsize. He and his wife didn't have children and they were delighted to see when I inquired about the house and I brought you and your mom with me."

"How much work did you have to do to it?"

"I added the rear wing, changed the compartmentalization, I rewired everything."

"Anyone else knows about this place beside us?"

"My colleagues, the other two."

"Do they know the exact location?"

"Yeah, but they haven't been here since the final version of it. I'm the only one with the master key." He reached into his pocket and pulled out a standard issue dog tag with a three keys. He put the chain over Alli's head.

"Now you have the second key. The first one is for the vault, second is for the control room, the third is for the hummer parked out back."

"What about weapons?"

He started to prepare breakfast as she poured a couple of glasses of juice.

"You know where my gun cabinet is. I turned the hallway closet upstairs into a small ammo stash. Everything is ready to go. Not just guns, other stuff too."

"Do you think that's enough?"

"My friend Chip, his daughter's got that part handled. He passed away a few years back but not before he told his wife to train their daughter to carry out the work. Suzette was attacked by a Sleeper and turned. Collette was their only child. She's got a place in the bunker when the time comes. She's also got access to her family's armory. I need to go there today and help her transport a load here."

"Can I come with you?"

"Of course. Just let me carry the heavy stuff. You got a baby to worry about now."

"So the people that hired you guys don't know you were translating this?"

"No. If they did, I don't think I'd be standing here cooking us scrambled eggs."

"Do you think the military's coming to put a stop to the zombies?"

"Sleepers. I call them Sleepers. And no, I don't think they are. Read the papers I gave you."

She settled down onto the bench and flipped to page one. "Is this happening everywhere?"

"Anywhere that storm's rained on is affected. Last time I checked, that storm front that caused all of this has gained in speed and size and was headed to Europe. So yes, this is worldwide."

"How can an ancient book cause all of this?"

"Something to do with technology beyond our scope then and now." He looked at her and pointed his spatula upwards.

"Aliens?" Alli asked.

"That was our guess. I wanted to read more but they reprimanded me twice. If it happened the third time they threatened me with complete memory erasure and a third one of these babies to scar me for life." He rolled his sleeves up to reveal two rectangular marks on his arm that looked like an equal sign. She always thought it was a peculiar tattoo design to get.

"What's so bad about the tattoos?" She asked.

"It was more like branding. And I didn't want to find out about the third one."

Alli thought it best to not push the issue.

"There's a lot of things we don't know. The knowledge stored in those books, that library in that facility could be the most important discovery for humankind. In the wrong hands it can be fatal."

"How can you come back to all of this after knowing about all that," she asked.

"I don't know. It took me awhile to adjust to doing normal things. Going to the store, fixing houses for a living, dealing with morning traffic. It all seemed irrelevant at first but then I realize how important the little things were because someone out there could just push the button and decide that it's the end of the story."

"We're gonna need more help to fight this."

"It's in the works. Collette is trying her best to form a local militia. For now, it'll be small scale. Conquer our little corner of the world. Then we'll go from there."

Chapter 15: Kin

Collette buzzed him in the gate and stepped out on the porch. She had dozed off on the couch when the intercom went off and woke her up. He identified himself as Cormac and she'd let him in.

She watched the white SUV drive towards the house nearly running over the solar lights that lined the sides of the makeshift driveway.

He's going too fast, she thought as the truck showed no sign of deceleration. She thought about running off to the side for a split second but decided against it as she stood her ground, picked the rifle up and aimed for the driver's side of the windshield. At the very last second the SUV swung around, sending dirt and gravel kicking off to the side, tires screeching then finally coming to a full stop barely missing the black pick-up truck.

Collette stepped off the porch and approached the SUV with gun still pointed at its general direction. She saw a dark figure in the driver's seat.

The last thing I need are Sleepers who can drive.

She walked up to the driver's side and saw that the figure was a man slumped forward with both arms on the steering wheel and his head rested on it. She could hear the engine still rumbling as she tapped the window with the tip of the barrel.

"Shut off your engine!" She hollered and waited.

The man reached to the side and switched the ignition off.

"Step out of the car!" She tapped on the window again. "You've got five seconds to step out of the car or I'm gonna shoot."

She heard the car unlock and the click of the handle being opened. She still didn't have a good view of his face. The door swung open and the passenger fell out of his seat and landed on all fours. Collette jumped back and she felt her trigger finger tense up.

"Stand up slowly with your hands up. No sudden movements."

I just need to see his face.

The man crouched and straightened himself upright. His face obscured with the shadow cast from his baseball hat. He held his hands up and swayed where he stood as if his legs were going to buckle from underneath him.

"Lift your head up. I need to see your face." She thought she heard him mutter something but was unsure.

He tilted his head up. "Please, don't shoot." He squinted and shielded his eyes from the morning sun.

Colette scanned his face for blisters and found nothing. What she saw was a guy in his mid-30s, unshaven, unkempt hair tucked underneath a hat, slightly disheveled, and from the smell of it, very drunk.

"My head hurts," he said to her as he leaned on the side of his vehicle. "I don't feel so good." He buckled forward and vomited on the driveway.

Collette uncocked the rifle and shook her head.

"Is that supposed to be freedom fighter number four?" A voice came from towards the house. Randall called out as he leaned on the door frame having his post-nap smoke.

Collette gave him an annoyed look. "I need your help getting him in the house."

"No way, look at him. I think he just spewed up his boots."

"I wasn't asking you for help, I'm ordering you."

He mocked saluted her. "Sir, yes sir, chief boss lady." He came down the porch steps and flicked the cigarette butt off.

Cormac stumbled forward and wiped his face with his jacket sleeve. Collette wrapped her right arm around his waist as he slumped his left arm on her shoulder. Collette held her rifle with her left arm as Randall came around the other side to pick up the slack. She felt the load lighten as he did so. She was a physically strong person but Cormac was practically dead weight at this state.

"He reeks." Randall complained as they helped Cormac up the steps and into the house.

"Let's set him down on that chair," she told him.

They positioned him in front of the club chair and let gravity take care of the rest. His hat had fallen off his head and his face was now more visible.

Randall and Collette stood over him.

"Why did you tell him to come over here again?" Randall asked.

"Because he sounded really desperate on the phone. He said he didn't know what else to do."

"What are we supposed to do with that?"

"Get him sobered up and we'll go from there."

"He's just gonna drag us down. I mean, look at him."

"There must be a reason why he's like this."

"We've all had a bad couple of days. Quit making excuses for him."

"We all deal with stress differently." She grabbed a throw from one of the couches and draped it over Cormac who was now asleep. "I'm gonna make some coffee."

"Um, guys. I hate to interrupt but I think we have visitors."

They were so busy talking about the new recruit that they didn't notice Sam enter the room. She stood by the doorway with Winger beside her who just now started to growl at something outside. They had forgotten to shut the door behind them on the way in and Sam was about to close it when she saw movement by the gate.

Collette and Randall walked to the entryway and saw three figures standing outside the gate. It was impossible to see for sure if they were humans or Sleepers at that distance. Collette got her net tablet from the side table and pulled up a live feed from the gate cameras. Sam and Randall stood by her side and looked over her shoulders as she zoomed in on the figures. The image was slightly grainy but it was clear that they had fully transformed Sleepers on the other side of the gate.

"Great. They probably saw his truck and followed him here." Randall glared at the sleeping man slouched on the chair.

"I need to get rid of them immediately. If others pick up their scent here we'll have a swarm of them standing outside in no time. Here, keep an eye on them and let me know if I miss someone." Collette handed the net tablet over to Sam.

"Need some help?" Randall asked. He already had his hand on one of his pistols.

"No, I got it," she responded then walked over to the gun rack and picked one out with a high-powered scope already attached to it. She stepped out on the porch and steadied her footing. She aimed at the first one and pulled the trigger. The gun shot rang but not as loud as Sam and Randall had anticipated it to be. Inside she heard the two give her a play by play description of the action from the tablet.

"Oww. One down," Sam said.

A click. Pause. A thud.

"Second one down. Just one more left and she's looking right at the camera now." Sam informed her right before she felt a sharp pain from her head all of a sudden.

Randall noticed her discomfort. "You ok?" He asked.

"My head hurts." Sam answered as she placed her hand on her forehead.

"Hey boss lady, something's wrong with Sam."

"Take the tablet from her," Collette screamed from outside.

"What!?" Randall asked.

"Just do what I tell you!" A frustrated Collette yelled back. She was distracted and had trouble getting her sights on the last Sleeper.

Randall took the tablet from Sam and took over monitoring duties.

"Come on, come on, focus." She took a couple of deep breaths and pulled the trigger.

"There went the last one." He used the camera to quickly scan for others but found nothing. "That's it. You got 'em all."

Collette shut the door and placed the guns back on the rack. Randall had set Sam down on the couch who looked like she felt better already.

"What just happened to her?" Randall asked Collette.

"That Sleeper was trying to get in her head."

"You mean like a telepath?"

"Yeah, some of them can do that."

"Why didn't you tell us before?"

"I did tell you when you first got here. I also told you there was a lot to learn about them. About all of this. Now you know."

"So how do I know if they're trying to get in my head?"

"A headache out of nowhere. Nothing like a normal headache. You'll know the difference."

"How can I keep them from doing that?"

"I'm not sure. Just try not to stare at one in particular for too long."

"What happens when they get in people's heads?"

"Look," Collette was in no mood for twenty questions. "I don't have all the answers. I know more than you guys but I'm still trying to figure things out myself. So please. You can grill me later. I gotta make some coffee."

**

"Oh look. Sleeping Beauty is waking up." Randall sipped on his second cup of coffee. He sat on a kitchen chair facing backwards, his arms placed on the backrest. All three of them have been sitting around the table eating breakfast when Cormac shuffled his way in.

"There's coffee on the counter, I suggest you drink a lot of it." Collette told him.

He poured himself a cup and sat on the vacant chair right across Collette. Sam was to his right, Randall to his left. Winger put her front paws on his leg and looked at him.

"She wants a pat on the head and a slice of bacon," Randall told him.

Cormac patted her on her head and took a piece of bacon from the plate in front of him. He took a bite then gave the other half to the eager dog.

"You just made a friend for life," Sam told him.

Cormac rubbed the side of his neck right behind his ear. He fell asleep on it wrong and now had a crick on it. His head still hurt but not as much. He noticed a bottle of ibuprofen next to his glass of orange juice and picked it up.

"You guys think of everything." He smiled as he opened the jar, took a couple out and popped it down the hatch.

"Not me, it was her idea." Randall pointed his thumb at Collette. "If it was up to me you'd still be in your truck covered in your own vomit."

"Sorry about that. Thank you for taking me in." Cormac pushed around the scrambled eggs on his plate.

"Just so you know, I won't tolerate recklessness if you're going to join our group," Collette told him as she spread jam on her toast.

"I understand. That was stupid of me. It's just been...crazy."

"So what's your story?" Sam asked.

"My wife and kids are sick," Cormac answered.

"That's a funny way of saying it," Randall interjected.

"Hush, Randall. Let him talk," Sam said to him.

"First, the twins got it and they bit the doctor so I locked them in their room. I left to get supplies and told my wife to rest and not to let the kids out. When I got back I found her in the bathroom bandaging bites on her arms. It's like she went crazy or something. I locked her in too. Shortly after, I called you." He motioned towards Collette. "It took me awhile to get here because I started to drink. You guys know what happened after that."

"How much do you know about what's happening?" Collette asked.

"Only what I've seen on the news and your videos," he answered.

"So you know there's no cure."

"Yeah, I remember you saying that. But you don't know that for sure right? The government or the CDC is probably on it already. It's just a matter of time."

Collette shook her head and looked at Randall then Sam. An unspoken signal to clear out the room so she can inform him about the events of the last couple of days as she had informed them. Randall and Sam excused themselves.

"Was it something I said?" Cormac asked.

"There's something I have to tell you." Collette leaned forward and sipped her juice. "I need you to keep an open mind. First, listen. You can ask the questions afterwards."

The two of them sat in the kitchen for close to an hour as Collette gave him an abbreviated rundown of everything she knew. He listened intently on every word even as far-fetched as it sounded.

"I know you have questions so ask away," she said to him.

"So if there's no cure then what happens to my family?"

"It depends. If they get out of the house they'll more than likely feed on people until someone fatally delivers a blow to their heads. If they stay locked up they'll eventually starve to death. But there's no telling how long of a time frame we're talking about. It could be days, weeks, or months. There's one thing to keep in mind though and it's important."

"What's that?"

"If and when they manage to free themselves from the confines of your home, they'll be able to make their way back to you somehow which poses a great threat to yourself and those around you."

"That psychic bond you mentioned earlier?"

"Ah, so you heard."

"Yeah. Bits and pieces."

"So what do you suggest I do then?"

"I'm not gonna tell you what to do with your family. I just went over the options you have. What you decide to do is entirely up to you. There's another option I didn't mention because I didn't think it would be a very wise one."

"What option would that be?"

"You can voluntarily infect yourself with the disease and be a Sleeper."

"Can't I just leave them where they are and wait?"

"You can. But you'd just be postponing the inevitable. They'd either starve to death or someone else will get to them and shoot them all down. I apologize if I seem blunt to you but I have to say things as they are. You've seen my videos. You've seen what I had to do to my own mother. I don't know about you but I did what I did for many reasons. I didn't want to see my mom suffer. I didn't want to see her harm anyone else either. She practically died when she turned into a Sleeper. Some of their memories linger after they've turned but it's more of a residual effect.

This disease only uses it to help them get to their next meal. I didn't want anyone else to end it for me. So I made my choice. It seemed to be the most humane way to release them." Collette's eyes welled up with tears as she spoke of her mother. "You see where I'm getting at don't you?" She asked him.

He nodded. "So I have to go back and..." He couldn't finish his sentence. He choked back the tears but failed. It felt like someone had sucked out all the air from his lungs and placed something heavy on his chest. He didn't think it could get any worse than it had been. He wiped his eyes dry and gathered himself together.

"So how do I make sure they're really...you know...gone?"

"A significant blow to the head is fatal. There's also incineration. Decapitation is not enough. The individual parts would still be able to function until the head is taken care of."

"If you want, I can take care of it for you when you're ready."

"No. I'd rather handle this myself."

"I can at least go with you so you don't have to be there alone."

"No, I got it."

"You have my number if you change your mind."

"So what happens after? What's the plan?"

Collette chuckled. "Everyone seems to be asking me that question these days. We form a local militia then fight for our lives. Regain a foothold of our little town then go from there."

"How do you do it?"

"Do what?"

"Keep your cool."

"Because I have no choice. I have to at least try."

"Can I borrow one of your guns?"

She walked him to the hallway closet. "Take your pick."

Armed and ready he stepped out front. "I'll see you around." He hopped into his truck and drove off. Collette buzzed the gate open for him.

"You guys had a nice chat." Sam walked in from the kitchen. Randall was right behind her.

"Where's he going?" Randall asked.

"Back to his family."

"Is he coming back?"

"I'm not sure."

All three of them stood by the bay window and watched Cormac's truck drive away from the property and disappear into the distance.

The uncertainty of the near future was never as apparent as it was at that moment.

Sam's phone rang in her pocket. Private number.

"Hello?"

A voice whispered on the other end. "Sam, it's Missy. I'm at work stuck in an elevator. Can you tell me what the hell is going on out there?"

Chapter 16: Breaking Free

"Missy! I've been trying to get a hold of you. Are you ok?" Sam lit up upon hearing her sister's voice.

"As ok as a person can get being stuck in an elevator with nothing but a pack of gum. I'm starving. Glad I took a piss during my break though. I finally got a signal on this damn phone."

"Did anyone try to attack you?"

"No. Why? You're freaking me out Sammie. What's up?"

"You really have no idea what's going on do you?"

"No and it would be nice if you filled me in. And then maybe get me a little bit of help here. I've been trying to buzz the emergency speaker but no one's answering me. I'm just hearing a lot of banging noises from the other side of these doors though. So someone's at least trying to get to me. I know in the grand scheme of things I'm just another customer service rep but seriously...a little help would be nice."

Sam tried her best to mask her panic. "The banging from the other side of the doors...are they saying something?"

"Not really. Just some muffled noises. I thought I heard someone growl. That was kinda weird."

"Listen Missy. You do not want those doors to open no matter what. I'm coming to get you. Just stay where you are."

"Calm down will ya? Why would I want to wait in here? You're scaring me."

"This is gonna sound out of this world but I swear to you I'm telling the truth."

"Spill it already."

"There's been a zombie outbreak and those things on the other side of the elevator door are trying to get to you to feed."

"Are you..."

"No I'm not on drugs. I'm not drunk either. I'm not fucking around Missy. This is the real shit so do what I tell you for once!"

"Ok. Ok. Ok. Geez. This place is guarded like a vault, there's gonna be help on the way for sure."

"I wouldn't count on it. It's every man for himself now."

"So what am I supposed to do if the doors on this thing open?"

"Push them down and run as fast as you can. If you can get something to hit their heads with, that would be a plus. It's their weak spot. Don't get scratched and don't get bit, or else."

"Or else what Sam?"

"Or else you turn into one of them."

A brief pause followed. All Sam could hear on the other end is her sister breathing.

Sam tried to visualize the lobby to Missy's office building. She had to show up there one day for a job interview. Her sister knew someone at the HR department and got a head's up on an open position. Sam was dressed in professional attire with a couple of copies of her résumé. The interview itself went well, or so she thought. She never did get a call back. She remembered four sets of elevators in the lobby. Two on each side.

"Which floor are you on right now?" Sam asked.

"Ground level. The elevator I'm in should be the one on the left side."

"That was my next question. I'll see you shortly then. You remember what I told you right?"

"Yeah. Stay put. If the door opens. Push then run. Go for their head to hurt them. Don't get bit and scratched. Did I get it all?"

"Yeah. See you soon, sis."

"Please hurry."

**

"There's no way I'm letting you go out there." Randall had been listening in on Sam's end of the conversation.

"It's not up to you. I'm not leaving my sister stuck there for those things to snack on."

"It's too dangerous and too risky."

"Since when were you afraid of danger and risk?" Sam stared him down.

"Fine. Then I'm going with you."

"Suit yourself. It shouldn't take long." Sam looked at Collette. "Is it ok if I borrow a couple of these?"

"Yeah, take what you need. There's more where that came from. You need a third person to help you out?" Collette asked.

"Nah. I got this handled. Someone should hold the fort down. Thanks for the offer though."

"You guys should try to get back before it gets dark outside. They seem to be more active at night. If you need anything just give me a call."

Randall already had his choice of firearms ready to go and was headed out.

"See you later boss lady. Watch your back," he told her.

"Be back in time for dinner." Sam cracked a smile and headed out.

Collette watched the two drive out of the gate as she buzzed it open. She glanced at the clock and hoped they'd make it back as they were.

**

Cormac arrived at his home without running into any trouble. He'd zoned out throughout the course of the drive, not remembering how he even got here. He entered the house guarded and unsure if his wife and kids remained locked in where he had left them earlier. He found himself standing in front of the children's room. They were still in there. Quiet at first but he heard them stir as they sensed his presence there. He remembered what Collette told him about the psychic link and what to look for. He didn't have a headache which was good. He continued down the hallway to the master bedroom. He heard Helena's low pitched moaning on the other side of the door. He placed his left hand on the door and the other on the holster. He released the pistol from its casing and cocked it. The gun felt cold and alive in his sweaty palms. The reality of everything hit him with a force that sent a rush in his head. He saw everything with a vivid sharpness that made him dizzy. The smell of decomposition leaked from under the door frame. He knew what he came back here to do but was now unsure if he could carry out the task. He bowed his head down and shut his eyes tight hoping that when he opened them he'd find himself in his bed cuddled up next to his wife. The kids would be up and watching their cartoons already. Any minute now the twins would run in here and wake both of them up. Then he'd have to get up and make French toast for the whole gang. If it warmed up enough the kids would spend a couple of hours outside playing while he worked on the house some more. Afterwards the children would take their naps which left him and Helena some alone time. Maybe crash on the couch and watch a movie. Maybe even make love.

Banging noises from the children's room snapped him out of his daydream. He thought he heard someone say something to him. Then the sharp pain on the back of his head took him by surprise. It felt like someone had taken a fork and was stabbing the back of his eyes. It sent a shooting intense pain from his head all the way down to his ankles that nearly knocked him off balance.

"Daddy why are you hurting mommy for?" Allen's voice whispered into his ears.

"Why did you leave us? We're so scared." Alice whispered to him as well.

Cormac tried to fight it off. He knew it wasn't them speaking.

"You're not my kids anymore, shut up!!!" He hit himself on the sides of his head as if the action would unhook the link between him and the Sleeper children.

"Don't you love us anymore? You never loved us did you? You wish we were never born. You'd be a successful writer by now. Not a washed up hack writer that's going nowhere," Allen told him.

"That's not true. Don't say that." Cormac shook his head and stumbled down the hallway.

"It is true. It's in your head. I can see it," Alice insisted.

Another sharp pain in his head sent him down on his knees.

"Mac, why don't you stop this foolishness and let us out. The children are hungry." Helena's voice tuned in.

Cormac covered his ears. "Stop talking to me! Get out of my head! My family's gone. Collette told me this would happen."

"It didn't take long for you to replace me did you now sweetheart?" Sleeper Helena whispered. "This Collette is younger and prettier than I am isn't she?

"It's not like that Helena. She's just trying to help me."

"You wanna fuck her don't you? I can see it in your head."

"No. That's a lie! This isn't real. This isn't real."

"You keep telling yourself that Mac. It's real. Your family's still here. It's just not yours anymore. They're gone because you're a lousy husband and father."

The words stung him from the inside and triggered emotions that he'd suppressed for a long time. Cormac stood up and aimed the gun at the master bedroom's door.

"Shut up or I'll shoot you. I swear I will."

Helena laughed. The children giggled. "You don't have the balls Mac," Helena whispered.

"You're an embarrassment to your family. I should've just married Toller. He's smarter, more successful and better in bed than you."

"No!" Cormac pulled the trigger and emptied the chamber into the door. One shot after another. "And stop calling me Mac. I fucking hate that!"

The rampage left him breathless. He let his rage get the best of him. He looked at the gun and tossed it to the side.

"Oh God. What have I done? Helena. I didn't mean to do that." He walked up to the bullet-ridden door and placed his ear on it. "Please say something."

Helena's laughter roared from the other side. "Pathetic. Always the pussy. Why don't you just run away like you always do?"

"Daddy, open the door. We're all better now. We're really hungry." In unison the twins whispered in his ears.

Cormac realized then that his family was gone. There was no changing that fact. He couldn't bear to let this illness control their bodies this way anymore. He had to put an end to this and give them the peace that they deserved. He had to get out.

He ran out of the house and into the shed. He dug around for something buried under piles of scrap lumber and empty boxes. He emerged holding two large containers of kerosene. He drizzled the perimeter of the house with it. He ran out of it partway but figured there'd be enough there to set the house ablaze and consume it in no time. He got into his truck and moved it further down. The last thing he needed was his only transport to burst into flames. He ran back towards the house and stood in front of its porch. This house was supposed to be a new beginning for all of them. A better life with more time with the family. More time to get his dreams back on track. Time had finally caught up with him this time. Now he's all out of it. He pulled a pack of matches from his pocket as he crouched down. He lit the match and watched the flame dance into focus as it burned its way down the stick. Cormac flicked it down towards a wet spot on the ground. He stood up and stepped back all at once as he watched the fire make its way around the house. The porch burst into flames effortlessly. He felt the heat intensify from where he stood and had to step back several paces. He could have stood there and watched it all burn down but it would soon be dark. He had to get back to home base. He sprinted back to his truck and got in. The engine rumbled beneath him. He adjusted the angle of his rear view mirror as he drove off the property. A thick plume of gray smoke rose above the house. The fire had engulfed the house like a giant fire breathing jaw.

"Goodbye," he said out loud as he made the turn down the long driveway that led to the outside road.

Had he stayed another minute he would have seen the Sleepers, all three of them, come out from around the corner, the back of the house and head towards the clearing for safety.

Chapter 17: No Good Deed

Alli spent the last hour reading the stack of papers her father gave her. She was in the den, in one of the old worn and comfy club chairs that's been there for as long as she can remember. She couldn't believe her dad would remember this much information much less have it translated from another language. For an ancient language it was straight forward.

"So what do you think?"

"Huh?" She looked up at him, startled by his voice.

"Didn't mean to disturb you. You've been engrossed in the reading material since you started. What do you think so far?"

"Hard to believe this is all real. If you didn't tell me about this and just handed me the papers, I'd think that I was reading a work of fiction."

"Yeah, it does have that otherworldly effect doesn't it?"

Alli nodded. "This is no fairytale though."

"Far from it." He sat across her and seemed very relaxed under the circumstances. That was typical of him though. Always remained cool under pressure.

"You see why I had to be secretive about all of it right."

"Are you kidding me? I would've thought this was cool back then."

"Yeah but you would've told everyone about it and had me committed to an institution." He almost cracked a smile. "In all seriousness, I wish I didn't have to hand you those papers to read. I would've been happy taking that to my grave."

"Yeah. But then I wouldn't be here sitting in the same room with you. I'd probably still be home with that asshole."

"You're right. That's one good thing that came out of this."

Beeping noises emitted from the black box underneath the surveillance. Something had tripped the sensors. Alli's dad looked at the monitors and there it was, confirming what he'd always dreaded. A couple of Sleepers hobbled across the yard and was quickly approaching the house.

"Shit! There's two of them outside." He sprinted towards a closet and pulled out additional firearms. He handed a couple to Alli. "You still remember how to work those, right?"

"I...I think so. How'd they get past the electric fence?"

"I don't know. I need to get rid of them first. We can patch up the open link after. Head out to the bunker. I'll be there as soon as I get this taken care of. Be alert and don't let them get near you."

"But I can help you."

"I got this. Head to the bunker and don't let anybody in. I've got my keys. Be right there. Hurry. Don't forget these extra shells." He patted his hands on a small stack of boxes that he set on the table.

"But..."

"Just do what I tell you."

Alli knew better than to argue with him. She placed the extra ammo into her backpack along with the papers. She tucked the smaller pistol into her pants and held on to the other one. Her dad was already on his way to the front of the house as she ran out through the back door, sprinted a few steps and ducked into the playhouse. She flinched as she heard a gunshot. She was tempted to go back out and see what was happening but she had to keep clearing the flooring to get to the entrance. Within seconds she was already in the lobby area of the bunker, watching the monitors and feeling helpless. So far she'd only seen one Sleeper down sprawled on the ground. That must have been from the gunshot she heard earlier. Her dad and the second Sleeper were nowhere to be seen. Somehow just out of view from the cameras.

"Come on dad, where are you?" She muttered to herself. "If you're not here in five minutes I'm coming after you."

**

Alli's dad bagged the first one. Easy. Right dead center of his forehead. The second one however, had a different idea. This one was smaller and quicker and looked like he was still in his teens. He moved towards the shed when he saw what happened to the first one. These things may be primal in nature but some of them were more cunning than others. Alli's dad turned his rifle's laser scope on and followed the Sleeper into the shed. He swung the double doors to let more of the natural light in. The sky had turned grey and dreary and although the diffused ray of light helped there were still shaded areas towards the back where a lot of the larger equipment was stored. Some shuffling to the left. He followed the sound which led him towards his workbench. There were piles of wooden crates stacked up by the wall that was tall enough to conceal a Sleeper. More shuffling came from around the corner. He held his breath and stepped into clear view and was about to pull the trigger when he noticed where that noise was coming from. A small bird lay on the ground with its broken wing flapping in an unnatural motion. From the corner of his eyes he saw movement to the right and he ran after it. He knew exactly where it was headed. Where he was going, there was only one way out and he was now blocking it directly.

"This is the end of the line, son. No place else you can go." He hollered at the trapped Sleeper. He heard a grumble from behind the cabinet as the second sleeper stepped out into the open. It stood there and just looked at him with an empty gaze, a red dot already focused on his forehead. For a split second Alli's dad almost felt sorry for the kid. He looked frail and helpless just standing there. Like he knew he was about to have a bullet lodged into his brain and split his skull wide open. Then the weirdest thing happened. The Sleeper smiled. Or something that resembled a smile. Stained teeth, necrotic gums and blistered lips kind of smile. Only he had a glimmer of madness in his eyes as he did so. Like he knew something that no one else did. Alli's dad pulled the trigger and watched as the Sleeper's head burst into tiny little fragments. He was too distracted to notice that a third Sleeper stood within arm's reach behind him.

Alli was about to go back out when the main door opened with a hiss.

"Dad!" She ambushed him with a hug.

"Missed me?" He smiled and hugged her back. This family was never the touchy-feely type. In times like these there's no reason for restraint anymore. It's all or nothing because in a split second you can be someone else's dinner, or even worse, become one of them.

"I was about to head back out and check back on you. Did you get them?"

"Yeah I got 'em."

"Good. Now we can go check the property for some holes. They must've torn down part of the fence or something."

"Just a sec. I wanna take a quick breather. Your old man's...well...old."

"What's wrong?"

"I just need to sit down for a sec. I'm kinda hungry." He walked over one of the club chairs and settled down.

"You want me to make you something?" Alli set her gun down on the table.

"Yeah, can you make me one of those instant noodle bowls that I like? Make yourself a snack too."

"Ok, what do you want to drink?"

"Soda's fine."

Alli disappeared into the kitchen for a minute and returned with a can of cold soda. "Food should be ready in a few."

He nodded and took a sip from the can. Alli walked back into the kitchen. He reached into his jacket and pulled out a small silver flask, coffin-shaped with a skull and crossbones design on the center. He unscrewed the top and took generous gulps of the whiskey. Some of it dribbled down his lips. He wiped it off with the back of his hand and placed the flask back where it hid.

Alli emerged from the kitchen with a tray, two piping hot noodle bowls sat atop. She set the tray on her dad's lap and took the other bowl. She sat across from him and sipped on the hot broth. He did the same. They sat there quietly for a minute just staring at their food.

"So..." She twirled the noodles with her fork.

"Uh-huh?"

"So are you still gonna head out to see Collette?"

"Change of plans, honey."

"Weren't we supposed to get more weapons somewhere?"

"We have plenty here. Not too worried about it."

"So this is it then?"

"You still remember how to work a radio right? I have a set-up over there for communications. And I already showed you how to work the generator. It's very important to run the routine maintenance here, you understand? Everything you need to know is in your room." He motioned towards the hallway. "The first door to the left. Files, documents, instructions, keys. All there."

"You might have to run that all by me again, I was never good at cramming," she smirked.

"Damn it, Allison! This is no time for jokes!" He set his tray down.

"Sorry. Just trying to lighten things up. I'm going crazy here."

"We don't have time to lighten things up. This is it. Just you. You have to get this shit right or there's no point in fighting."

"Don't you mean just you AND me?"

He shook his head.

She looked at him with puzzled eyes.

He took his jacket off and revealed a bloody patch on his right shoulder.

"No!!!" Alli stood up in disbelief and paced back and forth. "But how? You said you got 'em."

"I did. But one of them got me too. It was a set-up. I shot the first one down. The second one, just a kid, he led me into the shed. I thought I had him cornered. I shot him down but didn't realize there was a third one right behind me. I moved fast to side-step when I heard footsteps. Just wasn't fast enough. But I shot him down too. I went back in the house and grabbed a different jacket then I came here."

Alli approached her dad and looked at the wound which already started to clot. "I need to clean it out."

"No, no, no, there's no point to it. I'm already changing. I can feel it."

Alli wept. So many thoughts rushed into her head. How was she gonna pull this off on her own? She was not ready.

"This isn't fair. I can't do this alone."

"Yeah, you can. You'll have to." He pointed to her abdomen.

"I can't."

"You will. There are others. They'll get in touch with you eventually. For the meantime you just gotta hang in here. I hate to spoil the fun but I have to go."

"Where are you going?"

"Far away from here as I can. I need to take care of this. I don't really need to be infecting other people or eating them. I was never a big meat eater."

Alli sobbed. "How long before you turn?" She asked.

"Not sure. An hour or two. Maybe longer."

Alli wiped the tears off her face and hugged her father. "Sorry for being a fuck-up. I promise I'll make you proud of me."

"Nothing to be sorry for. That's life. I've always been proud of you. Now if you can work on that stubborn thing..."

"Never," she chuckled.

"I thought so. You're a good girl. A smart and strong woman like your mama. You'll be alright. Just read up on everything."

"I will." The well burst. She just couldn't contain all the emotions anymore. She sobbed uncontrollably.

"I have to go, baby girl." He felt a crushing pressure on his chest. He just finally got to spend time with his only child. So many things to catch up on. So many conversations that will never take place. A grandchild he'll never get to meet.

"I know."

He kissed her on her forehead and handed her an envelope.

"What's this?" She asked.

"Read it after I've left."

"Love you, dad."

"Love you too, kiddo." The longer he stood there, the more difficult it was to leave. He gently pushed her away from him then rushed out of the bunker and back to the surface.

She stood there, motionless, watching the monitors, placing her hand on the figure walking further away from the property until he was just a small dot from a distant.

And just like that, he was gone from her life again.

Chapter 18: This Wicked Life

The drive to Missy's work was almost an hour away with traffic. Without obstruction, maybe a half an hour at top speed.

"So what exactly is the plan when we get there?" Randall asked.

"She's stuck in an elevator. There's only one way to get her out and that's through the lobby. We're going to have to plow down the Sleepers when we get there."

"Wait – there can be a horde of Sleepers in that lobby. We have a lot of ammo but that doesn't mean anything. We can be easily overrun. We gotta come up with a better plan."

"Well, that's all I've got so unless you come up with something better then I suggest you just deal with it."

"No need to get so bitchy about it. I'm just being a realist here. I don't like bumbling around a situation, I like to be prepared."

"Being a realist? Really? Look around you Randall. This is as surreal as it gets. There's fucking zombies walking around. In Elmont! I hate to steal your safety blanket but this is my first attempt at a rescue, so I'm not exactly well-versed in the scenario just yet."

Randall's never seen this side of Sam as long as they've known each other. She's been mad at him before of course, but nothing like this. She gave him the silent treatment once, for nearly a week, because he stood her up on a date. Not on purpose. He just started a new job and was trying hard to impress his new boss so he volunteered to close one night and forgot about their dinner and movie night. There was another time where they got into a screaming match right outside of a diner because the waitress was flirting with him. According to Sam he should've *told that slut that I'm your girlfriend.* He apologized the day after even though he felt that she overreacted a bit. This new side of Sam revealed how tough she really was. Tough and loyal. It was comforting in a weird sort of way because Randall knew that she would do the same for him, had it been him stuck in an elevator somewhere. And that's the kind of woman you want beside you.

"Alright. I don't want to argue anymore. It's too draining. We should save our energy for important things, like getting your sis out to safety, ok?"

"Ok. Sorry, I'm a bit stressed."

"We'll go in there. You cover me while I pry the door open. Then we'll all get out and drive as fast as we can back to home base. How's that for a plan?"

"Sounds solid. Easy in. Easy out."

The drive down to Main St. was uneventful which is what they hoped for. No Sleepers spotted anywhere. Just abandoned cars, some parked right off the road and some in the middle of. Randall anticipated the worst as usual, but didn't say a word of it out loud. He knew those Sleepers had to be somewhere. Just because you don't see them doesn't mean they're not there. He's hoping that maybe they've exhausted all their food supply in the area and moved on elsewhere with the exception of the occasional stragglers. Stragglers, he could handle. A hungry raging horde and their chances go down significantly.

"Where to now?" Randall slowed the truck down as they approached Main St.

"Two streets down, turn a left, third building next to a hardware store," Sam motioned with her hand.

"I'm gonna leave the truck running while we go in for your sister. The last thing we need is for it to not start."

"You've watched way too many horror movies."

"Yeah well, you'll be thanking me later."

He turned left and slowed down to a full stop in front of the building. They saw nothing milling around in the streets. As for dead bodies or body parts strewn about – that was another story.

"You ready?" Randall asked.

"Just a sec, I'm letting Missy know we're right outside the building." She sent a text message to her sister then hopped out of the vehicle.

Sam cautiously made her way through the revolving door and straight into the small lobby, past the welcome desk. Randall caught up right behind her, gun in one hand and pry bar in the other. A leg was sticking out from behind the desk still wearing a security guard's uniform. Sam motioned Randall to stay closer up against the wall as they crept towards the corner where the elevators were. Sam peeked with gun held up to her chest. She saw three Sleepers clawing against the second elevator. The male one had a postal service uniform on. She could only assume that the other two were mother and child.

"Well? How many?" Randall asks.

"Three. Two adults and a kid. This shouldn't be so bad...right?"

"Yeah. I'll take down the dude. You got the other two handled?"

"I think so. The Sleeper kid might move fast."

"So take that one down first."

Sam took a deep breath and steadied her grip on the handgun. She snuck out from her cover but not fully stepping into clear view. The Sleepers were too preoccupied with getting to the other side of the elevator doors. She aimed for the Sleeper kid's head and was about to pull the trigger when the mother Sleeper caught a whiff of her scent. She tilted her head and let out a scream that sounded nothing like Sam's ever heard before. The other two Sleepers turned to look at her. Her aim was still good so she pulled the trigger and watched as the Sleeper kid's head jerked back. A second later he fell flat on his back. Everything played out in slow motion in Sam's head but the whole thing took less than three seconds. Sleeper mom wailed after witnessing the second death of her child. Sam froze as it advanced towards her. Randall pushed her out of the way and unloaded a couple of bullets towards the crazed Sleeper. The postman zombie was right behind her.

"Sam, snap out of it and start shooting!!!" He yelled at her.

Still shaken up, she cocked her pistol and aimed for the charging postman and got him right on the head with the first bullet. It took two to finally take him down.

"Shit. That was close." Randall grabbed Sam's arm and walked around the wasted corpse. "Reload and cover me. There might be others nearby that heard the shooting. We have to do this fast."

Sam did as Randall said. She could hear her sister's voice right on the other side of the elevator doors. "Missy, we're here, we're gonna pry the doors open and get the hell out," Sam said.

Randall started working on the doors. It loosened up fairly quickly with the pry bar. Missy got her fingers through the small opening and starts pulling on one side. The doors finally gave way and she stumbled outside. Having been out of touch from current events, Missy saw the bodies on the floor and panicked. "Oh my God. Who shot these people?"

Randall forgot that she still had no idea of what's happened on the outside. Sam grabbed Missy and shook her out of her shocked state. "No time to explain now. We have to go."

The three of them ran out of the building. They were barely out of the revolving doors when the audible noise of Sleeper groans came from over to the right. Randall pushed the sisters into the truck first and looked down the street. Just three stores down, a small crowd of zombies, maybe seven of them, had spotted the live ones loading up in the truck. Randall went around and hopped into the driver's side, and stepped on the gas pedal, clipping part of the sedan's bumper that was parked in front of them. One of the faster Sleepers bolted in front of the truck and grabbed on to the grill. The screams from inside the truck was mostly from Missy freaking out. She still didn't get it and thought that they had just run over a young woman. Sam yelled too, but it was more of her barking orders at Randall about how to knock the Sleeper off the truck.

"Shut the fuck up both of you!!! Sam, you're gonna have to shoot her from your side. You can do it, baby."

Missy's hysterics was getting in the way of Sam's cool. She had to do something. She grabbed Missy's face with one hand. "Sis, if you don't get a grip of yourself I'll have to knock you out and I really don't want to have to do that. So shut your mouth." Sam rolled the window down and held on to the grab-handle. She leaned out partially and shot the sleeper point blank. It was enough to loosen its grip from the front grills. The thing fell in front of the right side of the truck and the wheels made a hollow thumping noise as it ran the zombie over.

Missy sat quietly the rest of the drive home, visibly shaken but at least she kept her silence. Sam lit a cigarette and took a nice long well-deserved drag. She offered a drag to her sis, got no response, and passed it over to Randall.

"This is good, but I can really use a drink." He handed the cig back to Sam. "You ok?"

"I'm good. Crazy day, huh?"

"Yes it has been, and it ain't even over yet."

"You think your sister's gonna be fine?"

"I don't know, she's right next to you, why don't you ask her?"

"Missy? You with us? You're fine now. We'll explain everything when we get to home base."

"Zombies..."

"Uh-huh?" Sam turned to her. "What about zombies?"

"Zombies, they've turned into zombies." Missy muttered to herself.

Sam placed her hand on top of Missy's. She almost felt sorry for her. Always the last one to know about these things. "Yeah, zombies. That pretty much sums it up. Everything else is a big question mark."

Nobody else said a word during the rest of the drive home. And that was perfectly fine.

**

Collette paced out on the porch, frequently checking her watch. She'd occasionally scanned the perimeter with her binoculars. A couple of guns were on standby with additional cartridges not too far away. Staying prepared always kept her calm. Some called it busy work, for her it was a way of life. She always had to keep her mind and her hands busy otherwise she'd spend her time fidgeting, getting increasingly anxious then losing her focus. When she loses focus her temper gets the best of her. And that's one side that she'd rather keep under cover.

She heard the truck first before getting a visual of it. One good thing about living out in the sticks was that you could pretty much hear any incoming traffic before it actually arrived at your property. A quick peek through the binoculars confirmed that it was Cormac. She doubted his ability to carry out the task of eliminating his Sleeper family. To him, they were still his wife and kids. As she buzzed him in through the gates, she still wasn't sure whether or not he got it done. She didn't blame him for his hesitation. She only feared the repercussions if he didn't get rid of them. Somehow, they'd find him wherever he was which made his presence there a liability. This outbreak had forced her to do things she never thought she could have done. It transformed her into someone she hardly even recognized some days but it was all she knew how to be at this point. Her options were limited. Option number one: do nothing and perish. Option number two: Do something, and maybe just maybe, make it through this mess. She liked the odds of the second option better. It was as simple as that.

As soon as Cormac stepped out of the truck, Collette knew that he had carried out his task. His face was grief-stricken, an expression that Collette was all too familiar with.

"It's done," he said as he walked past her and into the house, leaving a faint scent trail of kerosene.

Inside, he slumped on one of the recliners. Collette filled two shot glasses with hooch and offered one to him. He raised his glass to a toast. "To this miserable fucking place. Where the dead outnumbered the living."

"For now," Collette added, and clinked glasses with Cormac.

"You wanna talk about it?" Collette asked, as she propped her feet up on the table.

"What's there to talk about? They're gone. I burnt the house down."

"Did they try to get to you?"

"Yeah, they did. They got in my head. They said things...hurtful things. It wasn't really them anymore was it?"

Collette looked down and shook her head. "No. It's not really them anymore."

"How'd they get in my head like that? They told me things without really talking to me. So not only do they eat people, they're telepathic too. What next? They'll learn how to fly?"

"Shit, now that's scary. I don't know how they're doing their mental tricks. All I know is that you can keep them out of your head if you really wanted to shut them out. Did you see the house burn down completely?"

"I didn't stick around to watch the carnage if that's what you're asking. All I know is that the entire place was engulfed in flames when I drove off. Isn't that enough?"

"Not entirely. You have to realize these Sleepers are resilient. There's a chance that they could've made it out of that. The only way to be sure was to stick around long enough to make sure they were really out of juice."

"Nah, can't be. I did some damage to that place. I don't see how they could've jumped ship without me noticing."

"Let's just hope you're right."

"Where's everyone?" Cormac just now noticed that the rest of the crew was missing.

"They went to get Sam's sister at her work. She's been stuck in an elevator this whole time."

"How long ago did they leave?"

"Shortly after you took off. I've been waiting for all of you people to come back since, like some kind of Mother Goose."

"They'll be back. That girl, Sam is as tough as nails like you. Can't say the same for her boyfriend though."

Collette couldn't help but laugh. She couldn't remember the last time she's done so.

A horn honked outside.

"Speak of the devil," Collette said as she buzzed them in. She ran towards the truck as they slowed down to a stop. "Next time call me instead of honking, you could be attracting unwanted attention."

"Glad to see us back, eh?" Randall answered back.

They all stepped out of the truck and hobbled towards the house. The stress and fatigue finally settling.

"You must be Missy, I'm Collette." She reached out to shake her hands. "I'm sure your sister's already filled you in on the details."

"Something about zombies. That's all I know," Missy answered.

"There's more to it than that, but yeah. For starters, you're right."

"Can we let her rest for a bit before we bombard her with all the details and freak her out some more?" Sam interjected.

"Oh, right. Sorry. Of course. Missy, you hungry? Got plenty of chow here. Feel free to help yourself."

"So what's it like downtown?" Cormac asked Randall.

"Over-run by sleepers, as expected. If anyone made it through the first wave, they probably won't last long down there. How did stuff go down with your family?"

"It went down alright. It went down in flames. I burned down my house with my family still in it."

"Shit. Sorry, man."

"Hey, not your fault. It had to be done right? That wasn't my family anymore, anyhow, right. I mean, that's what everybody says anyway. No cure. Just suffering. I'd failed them enough as it was." Cormac looked down, averting his gaze so that maybe nobody would see past the reddish glaze of his eyes. He wanted to be alone, more than anything.

"This whole situation is pretty fucked," Sam said as she popped the tab off an orange soda.

"Hey guys, things just got a little more interesting." Collette said as she walked in with her tablet device.

"What do you mean?" Randall asked.

"I just got an e-mail from some lady."

"Uh-huh, about what?" Sam said impatiently.

"It says, 'Hi, My name is Alli. Please help. I'm stuck in a bunker my father built. Our homestead is under attack. I don't want to be stuck here alone when I have my baby.'"

Chapter 19: Connections

"Too risky. We know nothing about this girl. How do you know she'll let all of us in?" Randall leaned back on the chair, his unshaven face worn and long from the fatigue and stress. He looked much older than his age. They all did.

"Her email sounded like she wanted company," Collette responded.

"What's wrong with staying here? The perimeter's safe with the electric fence. We've got ammo. We can see them before they can even get close. There's plenty of room and we're above ground. Who knows how tiny this bunker is? And what about the food situation? We could be locked down there, buried alive for who knows how long?" Randall was clearly adamant about staying put.

"Randall's right. I just got out of being stuck in an elevator. Last thing I want is to be holed up in a bigger container." Missy voiced her opinion on the subject in between sips of her tea. She was still visibly shaken by the turn of events but out of all of them she was the most sheltered one as far as exposure to what kind of threat they faced.

"You two got any opinions on this?" Collette shined the spotlight on Sam and Cormac. "Yay or nay?"

Sam sat on the counter. Her feet dangled a few inches off the floor. She'd been picking on some peanuts and dried up raspberries that Collette had put together from her stockpile. Despite Collette turning the attention on her, she refused to be rushed on any decision-making. She took her time and thought about the options and formed the words in her head first before finally giving her two cents' worth. "Depending on how big the bunker is, it wouldn't hurt to check it out. Those things out there...this...this is going to get worse before it gets better. As bad as it had been so far, I don't think we've seen the worst of it yet."

Randall shook his head in disagreement. "But what about —"

Cormac cut him off. "Let her finish."

Randall glared at him but kept his cool and bit his tongue for the moment.

"The electric fence is only as good as the grid. Then what? We'd have to keep watch a whole lot more than we have been. The ammo's good, yes. But we can take that with us. The stockpile, however, can't all be brought with us. There's simply too much of it. It seems wasteful to just leave that much supply."

"So you're torn, then?" Collette asked her.

"A little bit, yes."

"The stockpile won't do us any good if we're all dead from the Sleepers ambushing us." Collette unsheathed her knife and started etching something out on the wooden table. "We can be easily overrun by them or worse..."

"What's worse than Sleepers?" Randall asked.

"Desperate people trying to survive." Collette blew off the wood shavings and continued to dig and etch some more. "What about you Cormac? What's your take on this?"

"Doesn't matter what I think," he told her. "I'm splitting."

"What do you mean?" Collette stopped with her carvings and stabbed her knife into the table surface.

"I meant I'm not staying here and I'm not going to any bunker. I'm headed out on my own starting tomorrow."

"Why? That's suicide," Missy said to him, perplexed about his decision.

"I don't have to explain myself to anyone." Cormac chugged down the rest of the drink in his glass.

"What's your plan? You gonna go out and kill off us many Sleepers as you can? That's not going to bring your family back." Collette pulled the knife out and strapped it back down into her belt.

Cormac shot her a piercing look for the comment. "That doesn't mean I can't send those things back to whatever level of hell they came from." He stood up and pointed at Collette. "While we're on the subject, don't you ever mention my family." He scanned the room with rage in his eyes. "Don't any of you ever mention my family again.

Do you fucking understand me?!" Cormac stormed off, the sound of the front door slamming followed by the slight rattle of pictures on the wall echoed into the kitchen, breaking the group's silence.

"Did you really have to say that?" Sam said to Collette. "That was out of line. He just lost his family."

"We've all lost someone," Collette answered, unapologetic. "Besides, it had to be said. I'm not trying to make anyone's life any more difficult than it already is. Fight now, cry later."

"Why do you care so much about his feelings anyway?" Randall asked Sam.

Sam knew how jealous Randall could be at times. The last thing she wanted or needed right now was a petty couple's quarrel. "I don't want to have a fight right now if that's where you're taking this."

"Not trying to start anything. Just curious. He's a grown man. He can handle himself." Randall flicked his Zippo lid open and shut.

"All we've got going is this group. Each one of us contributing to whatever we need to get done. The smaller it becomes, the weaker it gets." Sam wasn't going to fall for Randall's provocation. She knew him enough to understand that he's just insecure and frustrated and he's trying to get a rise out of her. It was best to focus on their next move.

"The group is just as strong as its individual parts. If you have a weak player then maybe it's best to cut him off the group." Randall wasn't about to let her off easy.

Collette sensed the increasing tension between the two and wanted to diffuse the situation before it blew up into a full-fledged fight. "One more word from neither one of y'all about anything other than this pregnant lady in a bunker and I swear to my mother's ashes that I'll throw all of you off my property this instant. Right now, with you two bickering like this, you guys are the weakest members of this group." She walked towards the window, peeked out and scanned the view quickly. She saw Cormac leaning on his truck, back towards them, his head slightly lifted, looking off into the distance. An empty bottle lay sideways by his feet. She turned around to face the small, tired group of strangers in her kitchen. "No more bullshit. It's coming down to the wire. This place is secure – for now. It won't stay this way for very long. I've got several acres here and all it takes is one compromised corner for that safety net to go straight down the shithole. If it was just me, I'd be willing to stick it out here and take a stand. This is the home I grew up in. It's sentimental more than anything. But now that you're all here, there's no way I'm going to be responsible for anyone's demise. Before anyone opens their mouth and says anything regarding 'who died and made you leader' I'd just like to remind y'all that I've been preparing for this long before it happened. I'd also like to add that nobody's here against their will. You're eating food I've stockpiled, armed with guns I've acquired, in a home that's been in my family for generations. I'm telling you now, based on what I know that this place is not going to hold against an ambush of any kind. We might be able to fend them off for a little bit but only long enough to get the hell out of dodge."

"So you're thinking it might be worth our time to talk to this lady with the bunker," Missy said without looking up, still huddled over her cup of tea.

Collette nodded. "It certainly wouldn't hurt to chat with her."

"Let's do it. The longer we sit here, thee more time we waste," Sam said. "You want me to call her?"

"No, I've got this handled. I'll put her on speaker but let's not all bombard her with questions. We don't want to scare her off. Everyone with me so far?"

Everyone verbally acquiesced with the tentative plan.

"Hate to bring this up but what are we gonna do with Billy Badass out there?" Randall gestured his thumb outside the window.

"I'll have a chat with him after. Just leave him be for now. If I force an unwilling person to hunker down with us in a closed off bunker, it'll only make things worse." Collette clicked away on her keyboard for a few seconds. "There. I just sent her an email with my number. She'll either call me in a few minutes or not." She took out her cellphone and set it in the middle of the kitchen table with the volume turned up.

For that one long minute, no one said a word. They all stared at the phone, like they were willing it to ring with their minds. Collette looked down at her wristwatch. It's one of those kinetic watches that never had to be wound up or have its battery changed. The constant motion of the wearer was enough to power it. Sometimes, when she was alone, back before her new comrades had joined her, she used to look at her timepiece and think about how it would keep ticking away even after she had died, just as long as she had turned into one of those Sleepers soon afterwards and kept moving. She always got a kick of picturing herself as a zombie shuffling around looking for fresh meat sporting a $400 kinetic watch still ticking away. It was that sort of morbid sense of humor that occupied her thoughts as she continued her research, set out feelers and waited for others to answer her call.

The chirping ring of her phone snapped her back into reality as everyone else waited for her to pick it up.

"Hello?" Collette was unsure of what she would say. She had some idea of which key points to bring up such as terms and conditions of when and if they do migrate into this bunker.

"Is this Collette?" Alli's voice came through with a slight delay and some static noise in the background.

"Yes. Alli, right?"

"This is Spencer's daughter. Your parents worked with him about a project some time ago. He told me to get in touch with you."

"Where's your dad?"

"He's gone."

"Infected?"

"Yes."

"I'm so sorry."

"Me too. He told me to contact you."

"Tell me about this bunker of yours."

"What do you want to know?"

"Is it secure?"

"I don't exactly have any previous source of comparison, but yeah, as far as bunkers go, I'd say this place is impenetrable."

Great. All I need is another wise-ass to join our small but eclectic group. "You said you needed help. If you're so secure down there then you can just sit it out right?"

"That's not what I'm worried about. I'm pregnant. I'm going to need someone here..."

"None of us have any medical experience, if that's the kind of help you're asking for."

"She's not very good with negotiations," Randall whispered to Sam. "Maybe you should've taken this call."

"Nah. There's a reason she's asking the kinds of questions she's asking." Sam put up her index finger up to her mouth, pointed to her ear, then at the phone.

"No, it's not that. Just in case I don't make it through childbirth, I don't want my baby to be stuck here with me, you know, when I turn."

"So what do you propose?"

"My dad said to save you a place. He was real fond of your parents. This place is built to last with everything we'll need to stay here for a few years. All I ask in return is that you take care of my child in case I bite the bullet."

"It's a very tempting offer but I should tell you that I'm not alone. My friends are going to have to come too."

"How many?"

"Including me, five. And a dog."

"That's fine. This place is big enough for a dozen people. If you have any supplies that could add on to the stockpile, it would help immensely."

"Funny you should say that. I was going to bring as much as we can and load it out of here. That is, of course, if your invitation still stands."

"Of course. I don't want to be alone down here. I'm not looking for trouble either. But if any of you should start anything, I'm telling you now, I won't stand for it. This is my bunker and I don't need any drama down here."

"Fair enough. You mentioned that your homestead is under attack. How bad was it before you locked yourself down there?"

"I'm looking at them now. I've got cameras all over the property. There's about a couple of dozen scattered near the main house."

"You've got surveillance cameras down there too?"

"I told you this place was well-equipped. So are you in or not?"

"I'm going to need to talk to my group first."

"I'm in. Let's go for it." Sam was the first to step up and agree to holing down for a while. "Missy?"

"If my sister's in then I'm in. I won't last a day out here on my own."

"Fuck it, why not?" Randall caved in. "Maybe I'll finally get some darn sleep down there."

"I guess you just got your answer Alli."

"Good. Let me give you the details on how to get here."

**

"I heard you made a deal with the bunker lady," Cormac said as he stretched out on the couch.

"I thought you were asleep," Collette said. "And yeah, I did."

"Bad dreams kept me awake."

"You should come with us. Give it a try for a few days. If it still doesn't feel right after that then you can always go your own way then."

"I don't think a few days will make much of a difference." Cormac placed his arm on his forehead and stared at the ceiling. "What's the point of hiding out down there?"

Collette shrugged. "I've always wanted to live in a bunker. It's been a lifelong dream of mine. Now I can cross it off my bucket list."

"You ever just think that maybe we weren't meant to live through this? Maybe this is mother nature flipping us the bird for treating this place like shit."

"Yeah well, I'm not big on authority figures. So if this is what Mother Nature had planned for me, she can go fuck herself because I'm not ready to clock out just yet."

"My brother's missing out on all of this action."

"What do you mean?"

"He's an astronaut. He's up there right now."

"No shit? That's cool. I've never met anyone who knew an actual astronaut."

"He's going to have a hell of a homecoming party. IF they make it home."

"They'll make it home. Up there's probably the safest place to be right now."

"Huh. I guess it is." Cormac pulled the throw over himself and rolled on his side. "You should probably get some sleep."

"Just think about what I said. I figured we're not going to head out for another couple of days. I want to make sure we bring as much supplies as we can. Plus, I need to do something first."

Chapter 20: Follow the Leader

"Just went over the supplies again, we've got everything packed on this list." Missy scribbled something down on the paper attached to a clipboard. This was something she excelled at doing. She'd always been keen on organizing things which is why she'd been working as an executive assistant to the president of an accounting firm for many years now. It eased her mind to be able to contribute in this way. "I know we can't take everything with us but it sure is wasteful to leave all that stockpile behind."

"I'll lock it down. That room has a heavy door, pretty secure. I'll leave a few things on the table but that's it. Just in case someone breaks in here looking for supplies. They'll at least have a bit to keep them going just a bit longer. But they won't get their hands on all of it. When we resurface from that bunker, we can head back here." Collette peeked into the back of the small trailer attached to the hitch of her pick-up. "Looks good. Go ahead and lock it up."

Collette walked over Randall and Sam's ride. The bed of the truck was loaded up with weapons. "Take as much ammo as you can. Make sure you've got plenty on you too."

"You think that place is overrun by Sleepers now?"

"I think some of them have left but some of them might know she's in that bunker."

"You saying these things can still consciously make decisions like that?"

"I'm no scientist but I've seen a few that have made me question that, yes."

"Personally, I'd rather not have any of these Sleepers at all but hey, that's just me." Randall tossed an army duffel in the back and shut the tail gate. "That's the last of it."

Collette noticed the ridiculous amount of weapons strapped on to Randall. From guns, to hunting knives and a machete. "You sure you have enough there? Because I think you left an empty spot on your shoulder."

Sam chuckled. "I just told him the same thing earlier."

"Hey! You two can laugh it up now. But leader of the pack here has no clue how many of those things are waiting for us. I don't want my cause of death to be because I forgot to pack a knife."

Sam put her arm around his waist. "We know babe, we're just kidding around."

"Well, you shouldn't. This is some serious shit." Randall shifted his eyes, embarrassed of how jumpy and temperamental he'd been.

Collette smiled and shook her head as she walked off. "We'll be leaving shortly," she hollered to the couple.

Cormac walked toward her with a small army pack slung on his shoulder. "I'm about to head out." He looked past her towards the mini convoy they had set up. "Looks like you guys are just about ready too."

"I'm not going to ask you again. But if you change your mind at any time, here's the address." She handed him a slip of paper.

He placed it in his interior jacket pocket. "Thanks for your hospitality. Sorry I drank all of your whiskey."

"No worries. I had the good stuff stashed away." She walked him towards his truck. "Why didn't you get any rations?" She looked into his empty truck bed.

"I have a bagful. It's in the front cab next to me. I took some extra ammo for these guns and one of the machetes you had."

"Where are you headed?"

He squinted his eyes from the glaring sun. "Nowhere in particular. Just a little road trip. Take out some Sleepers along the way. You know, the usual."

"Take care of yourself Cormac." She reached out and gave him a hug.

Cormac didn't expect that from Collette but he hugged her back. It was the least he could do. He pulled back and gazed into her eyes and for a split second he thought about kissing her. Just to see if he was still capable of feeling something inside. The numbness used to keep the rage at bay had taken over. It was all he could do to not fall apart in front of these people. Now that he was about to travel alone, nothing would have to be kept under control. He felt guilty for having these thoughts so soon after losing Helena and he thought about what she had said to him back in their home. Sure, she was already partially a Sleeper then but he couldn't help but wonder if there was some truth to it. Their marriage had gone through a rough patch lately. It was something neither one of them really brought up but it was more out of mutual politeness and obligation. They danced around the subject and became very good at it. He'd never cheated on his wife but that's not to say the temptation didn't present itself once, maybe even twice.

She locked into his gaze. While he struggled to sort his emotions out internally, Collette was more of an impulsive, decisive sort, always had been. She'd been fond of him since their first meeting. It felt more like meeting an old friend you haven't seen in a while. They got on quite well and easy. She didn't have many close friends before the world decided to throw this curve ball on humanity. She'd only been in one serious relationship that ended months before the first Sleeper incident was reported. Maybe it's all the deaths she'd witnessed. Or maybe it's the after effect of this outbreak – the realization that lives can be snuffed out at any moment without so much as a warning. This was of course true before but having it in your face, all of the time, the urgency of doing what you can while you have the chance to had been more pervasive. She grabbed his jacket, pulled him closer and kissed him.

**

Collette did one last walk-through of the home she grew up in before leaving it. The rations they couldn't take were locked up behind hidden secure steel doors along with firearms. The chances of anyone finding that stash is slim. On the kitchen table were a few canned goods and various non-perishables. She checked her desktop to make sure that video she uploaded had already broadcasted, and it did. The only personal affect she took from her room was a photo album and an old book. Everything else was left behind. It was more of an inspection than a nostalgic walk, really. She wanted everything in its place because it was the civilized way to be. It was a strange request but everyone understood what she meant.

Outside everyone waited in their respective vehicles. Randall and Sam had their truck. Collette and Missy were to travel in the other one.

Collette hopped into the driver's side of her Dodge Ram and took one last look at the home before driving off. "See ya when this is over," she said to it before rolling her window up.

Missy handed her a two-way radio already turned on. "You lead, we follow."

Chapter 21: Underground

The drive to their destination was as expected. They opted to take the side roads to avoid any potential issues with large crowds of Sleepers and humans alike. They agreed that panicky mobs of people were just as dangerous. At least they were on the same page with that. There were houses that had burned down, either by accident or by intention, the cause of it was hardly important. Shops had been looted of whatever people could carry with their two hands. Cars off to the side of the road, broken glass strewn about everywhere, with figures slumped inside.

"Should we stop and see if anyone needs help?" Sam's voice came through the radio.

"No. That's not what we're here for. Besides, I think those folks are long gone," Collette answered.

Missy sat quiet for the most part with the occasional question, as expected coming from someone who was still in shock at the turn of events. "How do you think it all started?"

"I have my theories. Maybe I can explain everything when we're all holed up in that bunker. I think it has something to do with that rain."

"The one that lasted for a week?"

"That one."

"Then people slept so long and so deep, it's like they hibernated. When they woke up they've already transformed."

"So only people exposed to the rain changed?" Missy's voice became shaky and unsure. "I think I got rained on when that happened."

"I was too. I think it had to be a considerable amount. Maybe it had something to do with our individual composition too. Kind of like how some people can easily get sick but some people don't even when they'd be exposed to the same pathogen."

"So if it's like an illness, then there's gotta be a cure right?"

"I don't think so. Regardless, we have to stay alive as long as we could and fight these things. Maybe then we'll have a shot at finding some answers."

"The government should have a plan to get this handled...don't you think?"

"I'm not waiting for them to rescue me. As far as I know, Marshall Law is already in effect. But their uniforms don't protect them from being turned into a Sleeper too."

"What exactly is the point of hiding out in a bunker?"

"To regroup. Buy us some time."

Collette pulled up in front of a driveway with cattle fence partially open. "This is the place," she radioed back to Sam before hopping out of the truck. She pushed the gate wide open and got back in the truck. "You guys ready for this? Just take out as many Sleepers as you can. I'm going to let Alli know we're here."

Alli already knew. The surveillance cameras showed her everything she needed to know. Her phone rang. It was Collette.

"We're here."

"I know. I can see you with the security camera. There's only a few scattered zombies out and about the property now. Just drive around the back, you'll come across about five of those things. Keep your phone on speaker. I'll tell you if I see anymore."

"Sleepers."

"Pardon?"

"We call those things Sleepers."

Collette drove towards the back of the house and just as Alli said, there were five Sleepers hanging around. Randall took out three of them. Sam took out another one. Missy had her gun pointed at one before her hand started shaking.

"Just shoot him Missy!" Sam told her.

"I can't. He's just an old man." She gripped the gun with both hands now.

"He's not an old man anymore. He's a Sleeper. He'll take you out if he had the chance," Sam explained to her.

The old man Sleeper noticed Missy and began to shuffle towards her. Sam aimed for him but Collette motioned for her to hold. "She needs to do this herself. Otherwise she won't last a minute out there if we had to run." Sam hesitated but she knew Collette was right.

"Oh for fuck's sake. Come on, Missy. Quit being such a wuss and shoot already," Randall impatiently yelled.

"Shut the fuck up, Randall. I got this." Missy inhaled and exhaled out of her mouth. "I got this. I got this." She aimed her sight carefully at the elderly Sleeper's head as it picked up its pace, salivating and dragging his bum leg. With only a few feet away in between the two. Sam drew her gun and walked towards her sister just in case. Then Missy finally pulled the trigger, but not before she saw the old man Sleeper's face contort into an indescribable horror. His bottom jaw unhinged like a snake's to make room for his anticipated meal. His blood-stained teeth snarled at her. Then there was the smell of blood and rot and infection. Missy bent over and hurled off to the side.

"It gets better in time, sis." Sam patted her back then walked over to her sister's first Sleeper kill to ensure it really was dead. It was.

"I'm coming out." Alli's voice blared from the phone.

The group scanned the perimeter while they waited. Everything was clear at the moment.

"I'm here," Alli said.

"Where are you at?" Collette asked, turning around 360 degrees looking for her.

"Right here, by the playhouse." Alli stood by the entrance of a wooden playhouse waving to the group.

**

"This place is amazing," Sam ran her fingers lightly on the surface of the control hub, being careful not to actually touch any of the bells, buttons, and monitors that crowded its main panel. "What do all of these knobs do?"

"A little bit of everything." Alli leaned over and pushed down a couple of switches which changed the view on one of the wall of monitors on a nearby wall from a narrow shot to more of a panoramic perspective. "To be quite honest I haven't quite learned everything yet. My dad only went over the basics before he..." she found it difficult to complete the sentence. "Um, before he..." She held back the tears as she choked up. "I'm sorry."

Collette placed her hand on Alli's shoulder. "No need to apologize."

"Your dad must've been one great guy for having all this set up. A lot more than what my old man's ever done for me." Randall set down another box of surplus on top of the stacks they'd already brought down. "That's the last from our truck."

"He was a great man and a good father," Alli said.

Randall nodded in acknowledgement. "Lady, maybe you should sit down and relax and let us worry about getting settled in. You being pregnant is making me nervous."

Alli snickered. "I feel fine. I feel useless not being able to help you guys unload the supplies."

"Don't be. If not for your hospitality we'd be counting our days at my homestead for sure," Collette said.

Sam motioned at Randall to go with her. "Let's get all the weapons down here before it gets dark."

"Probably another hour tops and we'll be done," Randall checked his watch. "So what exactly is the plan boss?"

"Keep a low profile, watch the news, stay informed and have others join us get rid of Sleepers," Collette said.

Randall pursed his lips, not expecting such a straight shooter answer from her. "Well, ok then. That certainly sounds like a plan. So are we gonna be locked up here indefinitely?"

"No, I don't think so. Will we be?" Collette looked at Alli for the answer to that. It wasn't her place to decide. Besides, she was unsure if this place worked like a time capsule. To be sealed for a specific time and opened at a later date.

"No. Not unless we had no other choice. I'd hate to be locked up in this tin can for too long of a time. We can come and go as we please, if it's safe outside, of course."

"There are people out there eating other people. I think it stopped being safe outside when that happened," Missy said.

"How are you gonna get others to join the fight?" Alli asked as she tuned an overhead monitor into one of the few channels that continued to broadcast.

"I've been planning for this for a while now. I have a decent following. Plus I made a little recruitment video before we left the homestead. It's already out there, circulating. All I can do right now is sit, wait, and communicate as needed."

"So how much did your parents tell you about all of this?" Alli asked.

"Enough to get me to pay attention and help them prepare. You?"

"I didn't even know about any of this until a couple of days ago. I'm still trying to process everything. Now I have to run this place and figure things out."

"I've known for some time and I still don't understand it."

"This bunker was already here when he bought the place. He just made improvements." Alli looked around.

"I read some of the instructions. Your father sent me a copy. It's a lot of material to digest. We'll have to compare notes and get caught up so we don't miss anything critical."

"I hate to interrupt this very stimulating conversation but we're burning daylight here." Randall was already on his way out of the main entrance. "The faster we get this done, the faster I can have my supper. I've had my eye on those can of beans over there for an hour now." He pointed at his backpack on a chair next to a can of mesquite flavored beans.

"I've been expecting you guys to get here today so I prepared a meal for all of us for tonight." Alli walked over to the framed map of the bunker. "We do have a fully functioning kitchen down here. Or mess hall, if you want to be rugged about it," she joked.

"Ok, that's it. I'm working twice as fast. I'm officially starving now." Randall began his ascent to the surface. Sam and Missy were right behind him. Winger sat by the steps and watched his people leave, always on guard.

"Be right there," Collette hollered at them. "Thank you again for sharing your space with us. We'll all pull our weight around here, I give you my word. No drama. No hassle."

"Thank you for answering that email. I just didn't want to be here alone. Not with the baby coming. I thought you said there were five of you?"

"He had to sort some things out," Collette said. That was the best way of answering her question without getting too much into details.

"Well, when he's ready, he's welcome here too," Alli assured Collette.

"I better head up and help me before Randall gets his panties in a wad."

Alli kept a watchful eye on her newly found bunkmates as they hauled the rest of the weapons from the truck back into the bunker. She was initially worried about reaching out for help. She'd never met Collette before and she knew she'd have others who would want to come. There was always a chance she'd be inviting a pack of wolves into her safe haven. Now that she'd spoken with her face to face along with the rest of her friends, she knew she had made the right decision. Just a gut feeling. The kind you get when you first meet someone new. That voice in your head that tells you if you'd like to have this person as a friend or if you'd rather not cross paths with them again. Since this whole mess began she'd been relying on that gut instinct more and it hasn't failed her yet. She still felt bad about not being able to get her hands dirty up above but she contributed beneath by scanning the property using all of the cameras her father had installed. She had nothing but time since he'd left and she had used that time to familiarize herself with this bunker and everything it contained. She was by no means an expert on it yet but for every day that passed the more comfortable she felt in performing the daily maintenance for this place. Now that she had company, she felt a little lighter, even a little hopeful.

Epilogue

It's been almost a month since everyone settled into their new domicile but during that time the group had found their groove in terms of daily routine. It took a week to get used to the notion of sleeping underground but there were enough creature comforts in the bunker to make the transition easier. Everyone seemed to have found their own role within the group while still being able to function collectively like a well-oiled machine.

Sam ended up being the firearm and weapons expert. Ensuring that all the equipment inside and out were kept in good functioning condition and that everyone knew how to use each one. Missy became the go-to for communications related matters. Randall was the handy man of the group, making necessary repairs at the surface but also learning how the bunker's power source worked. Alli had given him the manuals and he'd been diligently devouring its contents. Alli's strengths were on security. She knew how to scan the area quickly and efficiently with the surveillance equipment. She had her father's good eye for details and the crew always felt safe when she manned that control desk upfront. She also insisted in doing most of the meal preps since it gave her the chance to do something normal. Collette was in charge of intel. Scanning media of all formats for any information and news and educating other survivors in hiding on how best to defend and prepare for the oncoming and inevitable fight.

As she expected, Marshall Law had taken place not too long after they had moved into the bunker. It didn't last very long. They had underestimated not only the amount of Sleepers they'd have to go against but also the capabilities of the cannibalistic and primal versions of these once human counterparts. The troops were overwhelmed by waves of attack that showed some semblance of organization on the Sleepers' part, which thoroughly frightened Collette. It was one thing to wage battle against mindless zombies with an insatiable craving for human flesh but it was another thing to have those very same creatures gain the ability to organize their actions. A flicker of logic housed in a monstrous shell with no conscience and complete disregard for life. That was the real danger. The ability to evolve yet retain that component that classified them as a Sleeper. Attempts by any organized government agency to put an end on the Sleeper invasion had been quelled. Once the initial public panic lost its steam everything seemed to have quieted down as far as mass hysteria went. Large bands of people dispersed and went their separate ways, forming smaller groups that either went off and hid, hit the road in search of that mythical safe zone, or for many, took their own lives to just be done with it.

Collette became more driven to get the message across. Thankfully the grid still hasn't completely collapsed yet and she took advantage of that as much as she could while she still had the chance. She broadcasted daily, without compromising their location. She pushed out as many videos to as many who were willing to listen. It was a difficult sell – to train, prepare, and eventually fight the good fight. But so far it seemed to have struck a chord with the small group of people that tuned in.

"These people really trust you," Alli said to Collette, looking over her shoulder as she answered emails.

"I don't think it's about trust. I think it's more out of desperation. Fine by me. Whatever gets them to do something. What other option do they have, right?"

"Let's see, well, they can NOT listen to you at all."

"True. I just can't see it all ending like this, you know."

"I'd have to say, out of many things that I figured would do us all in, being eaten by other humans was not on my list."

"I wouldn't exactly call them humans anymore."

"Part of them's gotta be."

Collette stopped typing. "Which part is that? You think you can sit down in front of one of those things and negotiate? They'd be more interested in nibbling on your face."

"You told us they were evolving."

"Evolving doesn't mean they're becoming more human. It just means they're able to organize their actions more. Their end game is still the same. With us being served on the menu." Collette resumed typing. "I just don't see how no one has stepped forward and explained to us how this all happened and what kind of solution they're putting together to end this."

Alli wanted to discuss the translated books but didn't think now was the right time for it. She walked around the couch and sat down just as the Sam, Randall, and Missy entered the lobby with Winger prancing alongside.

"I think it's safe to say that we're on our own."

"Ah, we walked in just in time. Another round of bad news please, says no one ever," Randall joked.

"Oh good, everyone's here. Might as well show you guys before I officially let this out into the interwebs." Collette hammered down furiously on the keys. "A new video. A call to action." She pointed to the middle monitor in front of them. "Watch that screen."

The image flickered as it switched from the usual news channel to a shot of Collette in her makeshift studio which was nothing more than her tiny room with a white sheet draped in the background to conceal all the metallic paneling behind her. "Hello again everyone. Based on recent developments as seen in the media, it looks like we're pretty much on our own here. For the past few weeks I've been making suggestions on how you can best prepare and protect yourself and most important, keep you and your loved ones alive. Based on everyone's emails and responses to me, I know you guys have been putting it into action. Most of you already know that the Sleepers are somehow evolving. This means we're going to have to shorten our training period to be able to organize attacks locally, wherever you may be. This also means you'll have to reach out and get more people to join you in order for our ambush to succeed. We have to catch Sleepers off guard but we also must know how to block their telepathic attempts to manipulate us. Do your best to implement the techniques I showed you from my last video. We all need to stay in touch with one another and keep our eyes on the ball. The longer we wait the more time we're giving the Sleepers to turn more of us into them. I'd say we'll have to make our move in a month, maybe two. I'll organize a meet up with those in my neck of the woods so we can all have a unified front. The time's ticking folks. I just want to remind all of you to prepare mentally, physically, and emotionally for what's to come. My friends and I hope to see you on the other side. As always, stay tuned. Prkrgrl85 signing out."

"Well? What do you think?" Collette waited for the group's approval. Although they may not be aware of it, their opinion meant a lot to her.

"I think it's good to go," Randall was first to answer. "But that's just me."

"I agree," Sam said.

"Me too," Missy followed.

"Ditto." Alli gave her the thumbs up.

"Nothing left to do but this." Collette punched in some keys that started the upload. Within a few seconds the video was up on her channel, which then sent out automatic alerts to her loyal viewers. "And so we wait."

**

The message traveled to its usual channels, fueled with nothing but its sender's energy and defiance. Its content devoured by those it was made for and those it was not. Those who knew of the early movement, it was essentially preaching to the choir, but it was what they needed to hear to propel forward and carry on with their plans. Those who weren't aware soon followed. Maybe it was the urgency in the sender's voice that set it off. Maybe it was just the right combination of words strung along one after another that tipped it over. For whatever reason it may have been, it was passed on from one source to another and soon there were satellite groups formed where there had not been previously. From sun up to sun down their days were devoted to nothing but preparation. It became their only reason for trying, for gathering supplies, for putting aside differences, for not clocking out early, for looking forward to the tomorrow to see what comes of this. They came into it with scars even before the first fight had begun. For many they had accepted that they could be faced with battling against whatever remained of their former loved ones.

For every person that decided to join the fight, there were at least a handful that opposed the idea and either wanted no part of it or wanted to fight the resistance. People who wanted to fight other people who wanted to eliminate the Sleepers. As if it wasn't difficult enough to kill the already dead, dissenting parties just made it even more complicated.

Collette and her fellow bunkmates continued with life at the homebase as usual. There were days when it seemed normal and peaceful enough on the surface to spend most of the day there. Then there were days where they couldn't seem to waste the Sleepers fast enough. It was all part of this new world that's taken over since the Sleepers woke up from their slumber and wreaked havoc amongst the living. This was now a time where you adapted or perished. And for the most part they adapted well enough to cope. There was no other choice but to suck it up and just deal with whatever was thrown at your face. At the end of the day, they all settled into their bunk, safe and secure, fed, and rested for the time being. Meanwhile, far above the surface, the storm clouds rolled in and cast an ominous shadow that turned the land a shade of grey, just as the first of the raindrops fell on the ground below.

End

www.ingramcontent.com/pod-product-compliance
Lightning Source LLC
Chambersburg PA
CBHW020326180626
46812CB00001B/73